Chapter 1

On the busy streets of London, a car with a mattress strapped to its roof zoomed past redbrick buildings and bustling little shops. A U-Haul lurched behind it, skidding and sliding over the pavement.

Inside the U-Haul, cardboard boxes were stacked neatly on top of one another. As the truck rounded a sharp corner, a box was flung onto its side. The lid flipped open to reveal garden gnomes, stone rabbits, and other lawn ornaments tightly wrapped in Bubble Wrap.

Suddenly, as if by magic, a pretty young gnome with fearless brown eyes pushed her face out from under the Bubble Wrap. She wiggled over to another gnome with a scruff of beard and a tiny scar slashed through his eyebrow. "Gnomeo, isn't this great? London! A new garden!" she exclaimed. Her red cap clinked gently against Gnomeo's blue one.

It was a well-kept secret that when no human was looking, garden ornaments could come to life. Everyone could move about as they pleased—as long as they didn't get caught.

"Juliet, you are so cute when you're excited," Gnomeo teased. He was so happy to be with the love of his life, moving to an exciting new city.

Juliet's brows shot up. "Cute?"

Gnomeo cleared his throat. "Did I say cute? I meant you're inspiring, dauntless, bold, cool yet hot—when you're excited."

Juliet smiled. "Now, that's more like it!" She gazed happily at Gnomeo. It was hard to believe that not long ago, she and Gnomeo's families had been bitter enemies.

For years, there had been a terrible feud between two old neighbors, Ms. Montague and Mr. Capulet. Neither remembered how it started, but once it did, even their gardens took part. Juliet's father, Lord Redbrick, commanded Mr. Capulet's garden full

of red-capped gnomes. Lady Bluebury, Gnomeo's mother, was in charge of Ms. Montague's garden, and the blue-hatted gnomes inside it.

When Gnomeo met Juliet, it was love at first sight. But it was a dangerous thing, for a blue to love a red. Lord Redbrick and Lady Bluebury's mutual loathing had led to the destruction of both gnome gardens and had nearly cost Gnomeo and Juliet their lives.

Realizing that their anger had almost destroyed everything, Lord Redbrick and Lady Bluebury had made peace. It was not in time to save their gardens, but it *was* in time to save their children.

And now, they were on their way to a new home, a new garden, and a new life! Gnomeo closed his eyes as he leaned in to kiss Juliet.

Suddenly the U-Haul hit a speed bump. Gnomeo opened his eyes to find a tiny gnome grinning at him. His blue hat had been sheared off at the base. "Wow, that was unexpected," said the tiny gnome.

Gnomeo slapped his forehead. He had just kissed his best friend, Benny!

"I can see why she likes you!" Benny turned and looked expectantly at Juliet's maid, Nanette, a porcelain frog with wide pink lips.

Nanette shook her head over and over. And then she shook it some more. "I'm giving you a subtle look that says, 'absolutely no way,'" she warned Benny.

The U-Haul took another turn and suddenly the gnomes were rattling over a cobblestone street.

"It seems we're going through some unexpected bumpulance, so, everyone, hold on to their Bubble Wrap!" called Lord Redbrick.

"Listen to Lord Redbrick," advised Lady Bluebury. "Whatever you do, however tempting it may be, do not pop your Bubble Wrap."

Pop. Pop. Pop pop pop pop pop.

"Benny!" cried Lady Bluebury.

Benny held a bubble between his fingers. Then he popped it. "I can't help it. It's a syndrome."

As the U-Haul jostled the gnomes, Lord Redbrick turned to Lady Bluebury. "I hope this place has a proper garden. You know how city gardens can be."

"Don't worry, dear." Lady Bluebury patted Lord Redbrick on the shoulder. "We'll be fine."

"Guys, why don't we all picture our dream garden?" suggested a gnome with daisies painted over his green smock. He pushed up his oversize

4

glasses. "And then that's just what it'll be!"

Everyone stared at Paris.

Paris blinked twice, pushed his glasses up even farther, and coughed. "I'm pretty sure that's how life works."

"You know what I want?" Nanette asked dreamily. "I want a massive infinity pool."

"And an even bigger box than this!" exclaimed a tough-looking doe ornament named Fawn. Pulling free of his Bubble Wrap, he used his hooves to shove down three tiny gnomes with red hats draped over their eyes. "Move, goons!" he growled, trying to make more room for himself.

As he spoke, the U-Haul slowed to a stop.

"We're here!" Lady Bluebury announced.

Gnomeo took Juliet's hands in his. "You ready?"

Juliet squeezed as hard as she could. "Can't wait."

"Poses, everyone!" shouted Lord Redbrick. All the gnomes and lawn ornaments froze in place.

Gnomeo and Juliet stood as still as they could. The van doors opened and a pair of hands picked up their cardboard box. They held their breath as they waited to see what their new garden home had in store for them.

Chapter 2

Mr. Montague and Ms. Capulet spent the better part of the morning and afternoon arranging the gnomes and other lawn ornaments in their new garden. They finally finished as a large clock in the distance was striking three.

Dusting off their hands, the two humans took one last look around, and then left the garden. The second they were gone, a rooster weather vane perched on the roof of the house swung toward the garden. It signaled to the lawn ornaments that it was safe to come to life.

As the gnomes looked around, an awful silence filled the air. It was true that they had destroyed their old gardens, but they were used to being in a tidily kept, well-managed backyard.

Now what they saw stretched out in front of them was an overgrown wasteland. Neglected trees and weeds choked every other living thing trying to poke out of the ground.

"Wait, where's the garden?" Fawn rubbed his eyes, but the sight did not go away.

The goons gathered around the stricken deer. "This *is* the garden, Fawn," they said.

Fawn groaned. "I want to go back in the box," he demanded.

Several small stone bunnies hopped up to Lady Bluebury. Using their own form of rabbit sign language, they twitched their ears back and forth.

"Bunnies!" gasped Lady Bluebury. "This garden may not be what we expected, but there's no need for profanity."

Lord Redbrick shook his head. "I'm not so sure of that," he said darkly. The garden looked very grim to him.

Paris gazed sadly over the scene. He had believed so completely that if he just imagined what his dream garden would look like—neat rows of flowers, a perfectly trimmed lawn with every blade of grass exactly the same length, a fishpond with bright blue water, a magnificent birdbath as a centerpiece—it would appear. Instead, he was looking at his worst nightmare of a garden.

A gnome named Mankini, who was wearing nothing but a red mankini, tottered over to a tiny puddle. "Look, Paris, there's a pool!" he shouted. He bent down and cannonballed into the puddle.

Mud sprayed everywhere. Paris pulled his glasses off his face and wiped them slowly.

Juliet looked over the run-down garden. She turned to Gnomeo with an uncertain smile. "I guess it's a . . . fixer-upper?" She knew it would take months of work to get the garden into shape.

Even though it was not what he had expected or wanted, Gnomeo was determined to see the bright side of things. He turned to Juliet. "Well, I think that it's the most beautiful garden in the world. Because you're standing in it."

Juliet bit her lip. She batted her lashes and leaned in toward Gnomeo.

Gnomeo shut his eyes, preparing himself for a first-class smooch.

Nothing happened. He cracked open one eye. Juliet was an inch away from his ear. "That was super cheesy," she whispered.

Gnomeo threw his hands up. "Seriously? I practiced that line for about ten minutes."

"It was like, awful!" Juliet pronounced. She gave him a sly grin.

"Oh, you are gonna get it," Gnomeo chuckled. He leaped at Juliet. She danced away as he began to chase her.

Gnomeo pursued Juliet around the garden, ducking under weeds and springing over shattered clay pots. They wove through a dandelion patch and ran along a picket fence with chipped white paint until they spotted a tall ladder against the far wall.

Juliet raised an eyebrow. "I bet there is a pretty good view up there."

Gnomeo flung his hand onto the ladder. "I'll let you know when I get there first!"

The two gnomes bolted up the side of the ladder. Gnomeo reached the top first. He leaned down and pulled Juliet up, then swung her around.

"Juliet, come down this instant, before you fall!"

cried Lord Redbrick. Even though his daughter was by far the bravest gnome in the garden (and had proved it many times), he still fretted over her constantly.

"When is he going to realize you're the toughest gnome in the garden?" Gnomeo asked.

Juliet grinned. "Now *that* was a good line."

"Didn't even work on that one," Gnomeo scoffed. He and Juliet turned and they both caught their breath. Below them, the overgrown mess of the garden awaited, but the view from the top of the wall was stunning. From there, they could see all of London—Big Ben, the London Eye, the stately Tower Bridge rising above the Thames. "Think of all the adventures we're going to have," Gnomeo sighed.

Juliet rested her head against Gnomeo. "Look at that view. We get to watch the sunset together every night."

Gnomeo gazed searchingly into Juliet's eyes. "Promise?"

Juliet smiled. "Promise."

Chapter 3

While Gnomeo and Juliet shared a romantic moment on top of the wall, a more serious moment was happening below them. As evening shadows crept through the garden, they passed over Lady Bluebury and Lord Redbrick, who were deep in conversation. As Lady Bluebury talked, Lord Redbrick kept shaking his head, but as the shadows lengthened, he finally sighed and nodded.

It was all that Lady Bluebury needed. She motioned for Lord Redbrick to follow her, and made her way to the center of the garden. "Gather round everyone," she called. "Choppity chop. We have an announcement."

Gnomes and ornaments formed a circle around the two leaders. Gnomeo and Juliet finally gave each other a kiss, and they headed down the ladder to hear what their parents had to say.

As he looked at the faces around him, Lord Redbrick cleared his throat. "I'm having second thoughts," he told Lady Bluebury nervously.

Lady Bluebury sighed. She knew how hard it was for Lord Redbrick—and herself—to be making their announcement. But she also knew that it had to be done. "For goodness' sake, we talked about this," she replied. She wasn't going to let Lord Redbrick change his mind.

"But we didn't know the garden would be such a mess!" Lord Redbrick protested. Even though the garden he had left had been utterly destroyed, he was still in shock at the dismal state of his new home.

Lady Bluebury shrugged. The situation was terrible, but she was sure that the decision that she and Lord Redbrick had made would make it better. She stepped forward to address everyone. "Lord Redbrick and I are officially retiring. We both think a new garden is the perfect opportunity to name new leaders."

Fawn pawed at the ground. "Oh no, she's talking about me," he moaned. He brought a hoof up to his face and covered his eyes. "I knew it."

Lady Bluebury shook her head at Fawn and looked warmly at Gnomeo and Juliet across the yard. "Gnomeo and Juliet," she declared.

There was a moment of silence. In the weeds, crickets chirped.

Then the garden exploded into cheers. Red and blue gnomes rushed to Gnomeo and Juliet, patting them on the back and offering their congratulations. The stone bunnies clicked their ears back and forth, expressing their approval. The goons formed a circle and danced happily as they held hands. Fawn gave a huge sigh of relief.

"Us?" Gnomeo gasped.

"Us!" Juliet said.

"Gnomeo and Juliet will lead us in preparing the garden for winter," Lady Bluebury continued. "When the garden blooms, will have a Seedling Ceremony to officially commemorate our new leaders."

"Yay, Gnomeo! Go, Juliet!" Nanette shrieked.

"Gno-me-o! Ju-li-et! Gno-me-o! Ju-li-et!" chanted the gnomes.

Gnomeo and Juliet joined Lady Bluebury and Lord Redbrick at the center of the garden. Gnomeo took Juliet's hand in his, and together they took in the sight—happy gnomes whirling wildly amid the overgrown vines and weeds.

Gnomeo squeezed Juliet's hand. "Look at this place. Isn't it perfect?"

"It's awful." Juliet was already thinking of what needed to be done before spring. She made a mental checklist in her head. *Pull weeds. Trim hedges. Turn beds. Find seeds. Plant seeds. Install centerpiece.* The more she thought, the longer the list grew.

Gnomeo chuckled. "It's unbelievably awful. But it is *ours*." He looked again at the vine-choked trees and runaway weeds. "New garden, London. We can handle this, right?"

Juliet looked up at her partner. A determined smile crossed her face. "We're Gnomeo and Juliet. There's nothing we can't handle." She was certain that she and Gnomeo were going to be the best garden gnome leaders ever. "Besides, what could possibly go wrong?"

Chapter 4

As night fell across London, streetlamps flickered to life. Far from Gnomeo and Juliet's garden, a tall, lean detective gnome wearing a flared tweed coat and a checkered hunting cap, stood slightly hunched, inspecting his trim and tidy backyard. He held a magnifying glass to a blade of grass, taking in every detail. If a human had walked by at that instant, the gnome wouldn't have had to freeze in place—he was already utterly still.

Suddenly, the hulking body of an enormous gnome sprang out of the darkness. He loomed over the detective menacingly. A sword sliced through the air.

Sherlock Gnomes ducked. He brought his magnifying glass up and parried blow after blow as the sword swung ever nearer.

Back and forth they fought, the sword biting away at the magnifying glass's wooden handle. With a well-aimed hack, the sword cut through completely, and Sherlock was left holding nothing more than a short wooden stick.

Sherlock slowly backed away as his attacker stalked toward him. Suddenly, he broke into a run. He vaulted off a desk and came down toward his attacker with a swift spin kick.

The attacker slid out of the way. Sherlock's foot hit a glass globe perched on the desk. The globe flew through the air. With a loud crack, it crashed to the ground and shattered into pieces.

The two gnomes immediately stopped fighting. "Watson!" hissed Sherlock. "Look what you've done to the globe!"

"*Me? You're* the one who kicked it!" cried Watson. He wobbled unsteadily in his bulky self-defense suit.

"Because you ducked!" Sherlock glared at his partner coldly. "The whole reason you're wearing

padding is so I can kick you! Quit your whining!"

"I am *not* your punching bag," Watson said.

"Don't be absurd," Sherlock replied. "Of course you are."

A wind chime with the cheerful blue face of a cow wearing an old-fashioned bonnet clanked noisily. "Sherlock! Watson! Just look at this mess! How many times have I told you—if you want to practice fighting, do it outside!"

"We're sorry, Mrs. Udderson," Watson said sheepishly. He bit back the urge to tell Mrs. Udderson that they were, technically, outside. He and Sherlock lived in a manger in the backyard of a redbrick apartment building. For years they had been partners, practicing their detective skills and taking on London's most vexing and complicated gnome cases.

Mrs. Udderson tut-tutted and looked pointedly at a broom and dustpan leaning against the side of the manger. Watson took the cleaning supplies and began to sweep up the bits of broken globe glass. Sherlock settled himself into a chair nearby and buried his nose in a book.

Just as Watson had finished tidying up, a trio of

gnomes stuck on a plinth hopped into the manger. "Sherlock Gnomes! Sherlock Gnomes!" they cried in unison.

"And Dr. Watson," Watson reminded them. "How can we help you?"

"Sherlock Gnomes!" the trio insisted.

Sherlock looked up from his book. "Yes, yes, what is it?" he asked impatiently.

"Our neighbors," began the first gnome.

"They've all disappeared," the middle gnome continued.

"They're all gone!" the third gnome cried.

Sherlock and Watson exchanged troubled glances. It was not the first time, nor had it been very long since they had heard of gnomes going missing from their gardens. Sherlock rose from his chair, took an unbroken magnifying glass out from the desk drawer, tucked it in his pocket, and nodded to Watson. Together the two detectives followed the gnome trio out of their backyard.

Under the cover of darkness, the trio led Sherlock and Watson through abandoned alleyways and deserted streets, being careful not to be seen by humans. Soon they came to a tidy, well-kept

garden. It was completely empty of gnomes. A few lawn ornaments lay scattered across the grass.

Sherlock bent down to inspect the ground. "Grass, perfectly even. Soil, undisturbed. Ant colony, thriving." He straightened. "Do you see it, Watson?"

Watson nodded. "Yes, there are no footprints—"

"Someone kidnapped all the gnomes from this backyard," Sherlock interrupted, "without leaving a single footprint."

Watson sighed. As usual, Sherlock had not heard a word he had said. As the night grew deeper, he and Sherlock bent their noses to the grass and began to search for more clues.

Chapter 5

A new day had begun, and Gnomeo and Juliet were determined to start making their London home as beautiful as could be. The moment the rooster weather vane turned toward the garden, signaling that Mr. Montague and Ms. Capulet had left for the day, they unfroze themselves and got to work.

Juliet had spent the entire night drawing up plans for the garden. Now it was time to put them into action. She directed the red gnomes to weed a patch of ground next to the house. When they were done, Juliet showed the blue gnomes how to turn over the dirt, preparing it for planting. While they were digging, she planted a whole bed of roses in another patch of garden that had miraculously not been covered in weeds.

After the dirt had been tilled, Gnomeo took up a shovel and started to lay down the fertilizer. Nearby, Juliet found a hose with a spray attached to it. She attached the hose to a water spigot at the back of the house, turned it on, and started to water the scraggly bushes that formed a hedge on one side of the garden.

When she was done, she went to see how Gnomeo was doing. He looked up and gave her a cheeky wink.

Juliet giggled. "You've got some dirt on your face," she told him. "Here, here, let me just get that for you."

Gnomeo smiled and closed his eyes. He leaned in—and got blasted with the spray hose.

"Did I get it?" Juliet asked innocently.

Gnomeo wiped his face, laughing. "Oh, you're definitely gonna get it." He dropped his shovel and chased Juliet through the garden, past gnomes planting new flowers and clipping vines off tree trunks.

Juliet was quick, but Gnomeo caught her at the

foot of the ladder leading up to the top of the wall. He was just about to give her a kiss when Benny came running over, dancing with excitement.

"Gnomeo! Check out what I found!" Benny proudly held up an old flip phone.

"Where'd you get that?" Gnomeo asked.

Benny pointed to a shed in the far corner of the garden. "The not-gnomes left a bunch of amazing electronics in there." He brought the phone up and snapped a photo.

"Take one of me and Juliet!" Gnomeo wrapped his arm around Juliet. The two gnomes grinned happily.

Just as Benny was about to take the picture, Juliet spotted Lord Redbrick uprooting some flowers she had planted that morning. Her smile faded as she watched her father undo her hard work.

Flash! The flip phone froze the moment— Gnomeo beaming into the camera, Juliet looking distractedly into the distance.

Juliet left Gnomeo and hurried over to Lord Redbrick. "Dad, I just planted those."

"They were too close together," huffed Lord Redbrick. Even though he had agreed with Lady

Bluebury to give control of the garden over to Juliet and Gnomeo, he still wasn't quite ready to give up the reins. He looked worriedly at his daughter. "Juliet, are you sure you're up to this?"

Lady Bluebury rushed over and pulled Lord Redbrick away. "You are supposed to be retired," she told him sternly. Unlike Lord Redbrick, she trusted her son and Juliet to know what they were doing.

"Maybe I should put off my retirement," Lord Redbrick said. "Just until the garden is up and running."

"Dad, I can do this," Juliet said. Her father had always been protective of her, and she cared deeply about him, but it had been a long time since she hadn't been able to take care of things herself.

"Juliet!" called Gnomeo. "Come on, we've got some unfinished business!" He held up the spray hose and glanced mischievously at her.

Juliet grinned. She was about to join Gnomeo when Lord Redbrick stopped her. "Remember, a good leader always puts the garden first," he told his daughter. Deep down, he knew that Juliet was a capable leader, but he was worried that her love for

Gnomeo would lead her to neglect her responsibilities to the garden.

"Always put the garden first," Juliet repeated. "Got it." She ran back to Gnomeo.

"All right, Lady Juliet. You ready to make a garden?" Gnomeo asked.

Juliet nodded. "I was manufactured ready."

Over the next few days, the gnomes worked hard on the garden. But none worked harder than Juliet. She weeded and mowed, planted and watered. There wasn't a moment she wasn't thinking about the next thing to do.

Juliet did not take Lord Redbrick's words lightly. As the soon-to-be leader of the gnomes, she felt the huge responsibility of making sure the garden came first—even if it meant less time with Gnomeo. As she worked harder and harder, the times when she could just relax with Gnomeo became fewer and fewer.

One night Juliet returned back to Gnomeo, exhausted by the work she had done that day.

"Hey, where have you been?" Gnomeo asked.

He had been working in the garden too, but Juliet had promised him that they would have time to spend together that night.

Juliet slumped into a chair. "Sorry, I got caught up in the garden."

Gnomeo pulled out the flip phone that Benny had found in the shed. "Well, Benny just showed me how to play movies on this thing. I got the scariest one I could find. Get ready for . . . *The Constant Gardener!*" He frowned. "Juliet?"

Juliet had already closed her eyes. She was frozen in place.

"And, you're asleep," Gnomeo said sadly. He turned off the movie. As he was about to close the phone, the photo Benny took of him and Juliet came up. Gnomeo looked at it—him, staring directly at the camera, and Juliet, looking completely distracted.

Gnomeo sighed. It was as if the photo captured everything that he was feeling right then. He laid his head gently on Juliet's and tried to fall asleep. But it was a long time before he did.

Chapter 6

Gnomeo woke bright and early the next morning, only to find that Juliet had already gone to the garden. He found her holding a goon by his ankles and thrusting his pointy hat into the dirt, making holes for seeds. "Hey, so, can we talk about the Seedling Ceremony for a second?" he asked. He had meant to bring it up the previous night, but Juliet had been asleep.

Juliet didn't even look up. "The Seedling Ceremony? Don't we have more important things to do?"

"Yeah, I know, but it's fun to start thinking about. I thought maybe we could plant the Seedling over there—" Gnomeo pointed to the far corner of the garden, but Juliet wasn't paying attention. She was too busy digging holes. "Juliet, can you stop for a second to look?" Gnomeo cried. He felt completely ignored.

Juliet raised her head and scowled. "Fine. I'm looking."

Gnomeo dropped his hand. "You know what, forget it."

"I'm looking!" Juliet snapped.

"I said, forget it," Gnomeo snapped back.

Juliet sighed. She loved Gnomeo, but she just didn't have time to listen to him. Getting the garden into shape was more important. She folded her arms and walked away.

Nanette hopped up to Gnomeo. "Ooh. That was painful to watch," she said.

"I don't get it, Nanette," said Gnomeo sadly. "Ever since we took over the garden, it's like she drifts further away from me every day." He knew that Juliet cared a lot about being a good leader, but it didn't mean that she couldn't have some fun while she was at it.

Nanette hopped up and down. "You know

what this calls for?" She brought the back of her hand to her forehead and pretended to swoon. "A grand romantic gesture! Something reckless and life-threatening. Something so dangerous that she questions your very sanity."

Gnomeo grimaced. Nanette's idea sounded like it was going to be very painful.

"I've got it!" gasped Nanette. She grabbed Gnomeo by the shoulders and gave him a deep, knowing look. "Go to the zoo and steal a lion. Then fight the lion in front of Juliet."

Gnomeo thought about it. As brave as he was, he didn't stand a chance against razor-sharp teeth. "I'm not fighting a lion!" he protested.

"It doesn't have to be a lion," Nanette said. "It could be a tiger, or an angry penguin. But you must rekindle the spark. I remember the first time you met. She was gaga over you." She sniffed. "Never saw the attraction myself."

"The first time we met!" Gnomeo snapped his fingers. "That's it! I'll get her our flower. If that doesn't rekindle the spark, nothing will. Nanette, you're a genius!"

The night Gnomeo and Juliet had met, they were

both trying to steal a rare flower, the Cupid's Arrow orchid, from an abandoned greenhouse. Gnomeo could never forget how Juliet had glowed with beauty in the moonlight. Or how she had looked at him when the greenhouse glass had shattered beneath her feet and he had lunged out and saved her.

Gnomeo gave Nanette a big smooch on the cheek. As Nanette wiped her face, Gnomeo went to find Benny. He found the little gnome kicking rocks into a mud puddle. "Hey, Benny, those gizmos you found—can they help me get an orchid?" Gnomeo asked. "The Cupid's Arrow orchid?"

Benny stopped kicking rocks and gave Gnomeo a big smile. "Step into my office," he said.

Benny led Gnomeo past rows of newly planted tulip bulbs and freshly turned beds and over to an old creaky shed in a forgotten corner of the garden. He pulled open the door and beckoned for Gnomeo to enter.

It was warm and dusty inside the shed. Gnomeo squinted as Benny shut the door, trying to make out his surroundings in the sudden dark. He saw

Benny jump onto a low shelf and pull back an old potato sack like a curtain. Behind the sack was a dingy laptop, two old cell phones, and a webcam. Benny had set up the shelf like a gnome surveillance van.

"Ta–da!" Benny said proudly. He pried open the laptop. As the monitor came to life, a photo of Benny and Nannette floated across the screen.

"Um, that was on the computer when I found it," Benny said hurriedly, tapping on the laptop keys to get rid of his screen saver.

"Yeah, mate. Yeah, sure it was," Gnomeo teased.

Benny dropped his head. "Right, image search," he muttered, trying to cover his embarrassment.

"Type in 'Cupid's Arrow orchid,'" Gnomeo instructed.

Benny slowly started to type. Four minutes later, he had tapped out the first four letters of "Cupid's Arrow orchid."

Gnomeo was beginning to lose his patience. "You have to hit it, just click it, just click the thing, you don't have to type the whole sentence," he groaned.

"Tell me when you see it. Tell me when you

see it," said Benny. He continued to type very, very slowly.

Gnomeo scanned the list results. "There!" he shouted, jabbing his finger at the screen. "That's the one. The first time we met we were trying to get one of those." He took over from Benny, and started clicking until he landed on a website of a flower shop. There, in a glass display case, was the Cupid's Arrow orchid!

"So we just need to find that flower shop," Benny said. He clicked on the directions. "Zero point eight miles. And looks like there's a massive blue line on the ground you can follow. Isn't that handy?"

"Let's do this!" cried Gnomeo. He was ready for his grand romantic gesture for Juliet.

Together, Gnomeo and Benny made a plan. Benny took one of the cell phones off the shelf and taped it to Gnomeo's back. He took up the second cell phone and dialed a number. Gnomeo's cell phone began to ring. Gnomeo reached behind his back and answered the call, connecting his cell phone with Benny's.

Next, Benny took his webcam and fastened it

to Gnomeo's hat. He checked the audio and visual outputs on his laptop. "I'll have eyes and ears on you at all times. You need something, say the word," he told his best buddy. He finished securing the surveillance equipment to Gnomeo with an extra roll of tape, then stood back, admiring his work. "All right, mate," he told Gnomeo. "Let's go liberate a flower."

Chapter 7

That night, Gnomeo waited until the other gnomes had gone to bed before he snuck out of the garden. Holding his breath, he peeked around the corner and into the street. There were no humans in sight.

Following Benny's directions, he scampered down eight blocks, hung a right, took three lefts, backtracked twice, and finally came to the flower shop he had seen on Benny's laptop. As he ducked into some shrubs, a voice crackled over the cell phone.

"Tiny Dancer. Come in, Tiny Dancer. This is Benny one-oh-one dash brackets, the Benlord, closed brackets, exclamation mark, smiley face emoji, dollar sign, dollar sign."

"You have got to pick another code name," Gnomeo moaned.

"There's no time," Benny said. He hit a few keys on his laptop. "Okay, Tiny Dancer, I've got eyes and ears on you and I'm definitely following you and not any of these seven other windows I have open."

Gnomeo waited for the foot traffic to subside outside the flower shop. When the coast was clear, he sprinted across the street and into the alley next to the shop. "Benny, can you . . ."

"Benny one-oh-one dash brackets, the Benlord, closed brackets, exclamation mark, smiley face emoji, dollar sign, dollar sign, yes?" came the voice on the other end of the line.

Gnomeo rolled his eyes. "Can you pull up the shop's blueprints and show me the best entry point?"

Back in the shed, Benny had an audience. Several gnomes had poked their heads into the open shed door and invited themselves up onto the surveillance shelf. They had gathered in front of the open laptop where Benny was typing away. "Yes, I can . . . no, I can't. Over," he said. Up on the screen, instead of looking for entry points, he had banged

out "sdfoijsods1146356f" into a Word document.

"Hmm." Gnomeo was beginning to doubt whether Benny was actually going to help him. He scanned the side the building. "I see a ventilation shaft a few feet up. Will that get me inside?"

"I have no idea," said Benny. "It might. Over."

Gnomeo sighed. He hunted along the alley until he found what he needed—an old, dirty penny half hidden under a trash bag. He picked up the coin, sprinted down the alley, and leaped onto a garbage can. He grabbed on to the grille of the ventilation shaft and removed its screws using the penny. The grille clattered the ground.

Gnomeo glanced around to see if anyone had heard. The alley remained deserted. He turned and heaved himself into the ventilation shaft. He wiggled down the shaft until he came to another grille. With a swift kick, the grille fell to the ground. Gnomeo jumped through and landed as quietly as he could. "All right, I'm in," he whispered.

"Nice work, Tiny Dancer!" Benny cheered. He closed three browsers on his screen and brought the webcam view onto the laptop. He could see flower bouquets and garden plants arranged on three-tiered stands and inside glass display cases. He could also see red sensor beams moving over every surface. "Okay, those red beams must be the burglar alarm," said Benny. "What's your plan, Tiny D?"

Gnomeo shrugged his shoulders. "Oh, just the usual, totally gonna wing it, risk life and limb, escape by the skin of my teeth. I call it, 'pulling a Gnomeo.'" He paused. "And don't call me Tiny D."

Gathering up his energy, he vaulted across the shop, barely missing the motion detector beams. He hurried over to the display case where the Cupid's Arrow orchid was. He shook the door. "The case— it's locked!" he said.

"Do you have a rocket-powered grenade launcher, Tiny Dancer?" Benny asked.

Gnomeo groaned. "Seriously?"

"Oh. Well then just find a paper clip, jam it in the lock, and wiggle it around a bit."

"All right," said Gnomeo doubtfully. He looked carefully around him. Up on the counter next to the cash register, he could see a dish full of thumb-tacks, rubber bands—and paper clips!

Dodging and weaving past the motion sensor beams, Gnomeo made it to the counter. He

hopped up onto a chair and sprang up once more, landing on the counter. He plucked a paper clip up from the dish and returned to the display case. He unbent the paper clip until it was a long thin wire then jammed it into the lock. After a few jimmies, the lock popped open. Gnomeo had done it!

Back in the shed, Benny and the gnomes were glued to the laptop. "Huh, I can't believe that worked!" Benny said.

"Hey, Benny," called a voice.

Benny whirled around. It was Juliet!

"Have you seen Gnomeo?" she asked.

"No . . . well . . . maybe." Benny winced.

Juliet glanced at the laptop and saw Gnomeo delicately lifting the Cupid's Arrow orchid out of its vase. "Is that Gnomeo?" she gasped. "Where is he? What is he doing?"

Gnomeo heard Juliet's voice over the cell phone. He swung around and the webcam on his hat hit the vase, knocking it off the shelf.

"No!" Gnomeo cried. He reached out and barely managed to grab the vase before it plummeted to the ground. He wiped his forehead and heaved a sigh of relief.

Behind him, the plinth holding the vase began to topple.

Gnomeo turned just in time to see the plinth tip off the display case. With a horrendous crack, it hit the floor and broke into a thousand pieces.

The burglar alarm began to wail.

"Oh, fertilizer." Holding the Cupid's Arrow orchid, Gnomeo leaped down from the display case. He skirted past the shattered plinth, making a beeline for the ventilation shaft. When he reached it, he jumped up—but the shaft opening was too high!

Outside the shop, sirens blared, and blue and white lights flashed as a police car pulled up. Gnomeo saw the silhouettes of two officers heading toward the front door. "Next time, remember to have an escape plan," he told himself. "If there is a next time." He took a deep breath, gathered up his strength, and made a second jump to reach the shaft.

Gnomeo bonked against the wall and tumbled back down. It was no use. He wasn't going to make it. He turned toward the entrance of the flower shop. He could see the policemen rattling at the lock.

Gnomeo froze. In seconds, he would be discovered and his quest for the Cupid's Arrow orchid would come to a horrible end.

Suddenly, a familiar face popped out of the ventilation shaft.

"Juliet!" shouted Gnomeo.

Juliet held her hand out to Gnomeo. "Hurry!" she cried.

Gnomeo took a running leap and grabbed on to Juliet's outstretched hand. She yanked him through the vent just as the police burst inside.

Chapter 8

On the rooftop of a London row house a few miles away, Sherlock and Watson surveyed yet another empty garden.

"Another garden of gnomes disappears without a trace." Sherlock stroked his chin.

Watson unscrewed the bottom of his cane. He pulled out a rolled-up map and smoothed it out. It showed the city streets of London, with Xs marked where each of the gnomes had disappeared from their gardens.

Watson dug into his waistcoat pocket and found a pen. On the map, he located the garden where he and Sherlock were standing, and drew another X.

"This makes eight gardens in one week," he said.

"Eight gardens of gnomes vanish into thin air. No clues, not so much as a single footprint." Sherlock gazed darkly over the abandoned garden. He had a hunch as to who was responsible for the gnome disappearances. "There's only one ornament who could pull off such a diabolical scheme."

In the distance, thunder rumbled.

"Moriarty," Sherlock pronounced. He spoke the name as though it was a horrible curse.

Watson shuddered. "But Moriarty's dead," he said.

Sherlock did not respond.

"And Moriarty never did anything this big before." Watson studied the map with the ominous Xs, searching for clues.

"Yes, yes. And Moriarty would have left something for me. Something to indicate that this is his handiwork. What am I missing?" Sherlock paced along the garden wall as storm clouds gathered overhead. Suddenly, his eyes gleamed. "Watson, give me your map—quickly now. Those gnomes that just moved in. Where do they live?"

"Right here." Watson showed Sherlock a spot

on the map. Sherlock nodded his head. "Do you see, Watson? Moriarty *has* left his calling card! If they're the next target . . ." He snatched the pen out of Watson's hand and marked a final *X* on the map.

To complete a giant letter *M* spanning all of London, the next gnome garden to disappear would have to be the one that had been moved into a few days ago. One that was nowhere near ready for winter.

Gnomeo and Juliet's garden.

"Hurry, Watson!" Sherlock commanded. He sprang toward the edge of the garden. "Those gnomes are in terrible danger!"

As Sherlock and Watson raced across the rooftops of London, Gnomeo and Juliet were running too. After Juliet had saved Gnomeo, they had crawled through the vent and exited the flower shop, and were now heading full speed down the alleyway, getting as far away from the crime scene as possible.

But even when were safely several blocks away, Juliet kept running.

"Juliet, wait. Stop. I can explain—" panted Gnomeo.

Juliet whirled around, her hands on her hips. "What on earth were you thinking?" she cried.

Gnomeo knew he had to save his grand romantic gesture—and fast. He held up the Cupid's Arrow orchid. "I was getting this." He looked deeply into Juliet's eyes. He willed her to recognize the beautiful thing that had brought them together not so long ago. "Remember this?"

"You risked getting smashed for some flower?" Juliet yelled.

Gnomeo staggered back, hurt. "Not *some* flower!" he shouted. "*Our* flower! I did this for you!"

"You did this for me?" Juliet asked incredulously. She brought her fingers up to her temples and rubbed them. "For me? I've got responsibilities! I don't have time for this!"

Gnomeo shook his head. "No. You just don't have time for *us*. All you seem to care about is the garden!"

Juliet folded her arms. "We're the leaders, Gnomeo. We are supposed to take care of it! Don't you care about *that*?"

"I do care," Gnomeo protested, "but we're allowed to have fun, too."

"No one's stopping you from having fun!" Juliet shouted.

Gnomeo took Juliet's hands in his own. "Juliet, I want to have fun with *you*. I want *us* to have adventures *together*."

Juliet pulled away. "There will be plenty of time for fun and adventure *after* I get the garden ready." She remembered the words her father had told her when they had first arrived in their new home. "A good leader always puts the garden first."

"Unbelievable!" Gnomeo snorted. "What do you care more about: the garden or me?"

Juliet raised her eyebrows. "Oh, you're being ridiculous."

"That's not an answer," said Gnomeo.

Juliet had had it with Gnomeo, with his romantic gesture, with his dangerous selfish acts—all of it. "The garden can't wait," she told Gnomeo coldly. *"And you can."*

Gnomeo stared at Juliet, shocked. He could feel his heart cracking.

The cell phone crackled to life. "Gnomeo! Help!" screamed Benny. "There's something here! It's a—AAHHHH!!!"

Gnomeo wrenched the cell phone from his back and held it to his mouth. "Benny! What's going on?"

There was static.

"Benny? Benny!" Gnomeo shouted.

Nothing. The line had gone dead.

Chapter 9

Wordlessly Gnomeo and Juliet raced across the back alleyways of London. They dodged garbage cans and stray cats, rushing homeward as fast as they could. They rounded a final corner and burst into the garden, both of them gasping for air.

It was empty. The only movement was a swirl of dead leaves over a patch of bare ground.

Gnomeo ran to the shed. The door was open, hanging crookedly from the hinges. Something gigantic had ripped it half off. Benny was nowhere to be seen.

"Dad! Nanette!" Juliet shouted.

"Benny! Mom!" Gnomeo called. He turned to

Juliet. "Nobody is here. They're all gone!"

Juliet covered her face with her hands. The garden was her responsibility. But now, because she had to go and save Gnomeo, she had let everyone else down.

As she tried to think what to do next, two shadows swooped through the air. Sherlock and Watson leaped from a rooftop and landed on the garden wall. Finding the ladder, they hastily climbed down.

Sherlock surveyed the scene and frowned. "We're too late."

Watson shooed Gnomeo and Juliet toward the garden gate. "Please step back. This is an active crime scene." He dropped to the ground and started to look for footprints. Sherlock studied the angle of the shed door, and then knocked on the bottom hinge.

The door peeled completely off the hinge and crashed into the dirt.

"Hey!" Juliet protested. She did not like the fact that two strangers—one tall and thin with a tiny goatee, the other short and plump with a mutton-chop mustache—had dropped into the garden without an invitation. "Who are you, and what are you doing in our garden? Identify yourselves, please."

Watson looked up from inspecting the ground. "*Your* garden? Where were the two of you when this happened?" he asked.

Juliet glared at Gnomeo. Where had they been, indeed!

"They were having a lovers' quarrel," explained Sherlock. "See how she's facing away from him? She's angry with him. The flower in his hand was intended as a romantic gesture—a desperate act that predictably backfired."

"Ugh," said Gnomeo. Even though the tall gnome with the hunting cap was right, it still didn't feel good to be reminded of his failed plan.

"Watson, search the west quadrant," Sherlock ordered. "If that fiend is behind this, he will have left a clue."

Juliet saw something lying on the ground. She bent down and picked it up. It was a card with an *M* written on it, and a photograph of a *9*. "What's this?" she asked.

Sherlock strode over. "Give that to me!"

Juliet shook her head and held the card behind her back. "Tell me what it is."

"It's a clue," said Sherlock, annoyed. "It will lead us to our next destination. And if you ever want to see your friends and family again, you'll hand it over!"

Juliet reluctantly gave the card to Sherlock. He inspected the card and the photograph. "The *9*—there's a slight crack in its leg. Where have I seen this particular *9* before?"

The detective closed his eyes and dove into his mind palace. It was a complicated mental library of filing cabinets that systematically categorized every piece of information he had ever gathered. "Nine," he muttered. "Nine, nine, nine, nine, nine, nine, nine, nine, nine." An image of a store popped into his head, with a red *9* painted on its door. He snapped his head up. "Nine! I've got it! To Chinatown, Watson," he called. "The game is afoot."

Gnomeo folded his arms. "Mate, you're going nowhere until you tell us what you know." He grabbed Sherlock's elbow—only to be neatly flipped onto his backside by the detective.

As Sherlock strode out of the garden, Watson touched the brim of his bowler cap apologetically at Gnomeo. "Stay here! We're on the case." He took off running after Sherlock.

Gnomeo couldn't believe it. "What a complete and total—"

Juliet hurried by him. "Get up. We're going after them." She darted after Sherlock and Watson. "Wait! Hold on! Wait!" she called.

Gnomeo got to his feet. "And now we're running after him," he said with a sigh. Shaking his head, he took after Juliet.

Chapter 10

Gnomeo and Juliet followed Sherlock and Watson through the streets of London. Every so often, they had to freeze in place when a human came into view. Just when they had nearly caught up to the two detectives, Watson flipped open the top of his cane. He pressed a remote-control switch, and a manhole cover appeared out of nowhere. It slid silently open, revealing the sewage system underneath.

Without breaking stride, Watson and Sherlock plunged into the darkness below.

Juliet ran toward the manhole and leaped down into the sewer.

"Whoa!" Gnomeo held back. Then, as Juliet disappeared from view, he sighed, took a deep breath, plugged his nose, and jumped in after her.

It was cold and wet. Gooey blobs of slime drifted by, and Gnomeo nearly gagged. He heard the sound of splashing, and saw Sherlock and Watson climbing into a boat. On the back was a fan crusted over with dirt. Sherlock turned it on, and the blades began to whirl. The boat skated across the water.

A shadow crossed in front of him, and Gnomeo saw Juliet run toward the boat. He had no choice but to follow.

They chased the boat through the twisty tunnels, always a few steps behind the two detectives. The water grew shallower and shallower, though the stench remained the same.

"Wait, wait please!" Juliet cried.

"All ahead full, Watson!" Sherlock's voice echoed off the tunnel walls. There was a click. The whirring of the fan grew more frantic.

Gnomeo grabbed Juliet's elbow as she skidded around a corner. "Forget them!" he panted. "We can handle this ourselves."

Juliet shook herself free and continued to chase Sherlock and Watson.

Gnomeo gritted his teeth. "Or do the exact opposite. Your call." After a few more turns, they came to a long stretch of tunnel. The boat was at the end of it.

Sherlock ramped up the speed of the fan even more. Using a spoon as a rudder, Watson banked hard to the left to avoid a pile of sludge, and nearly rammed into a pile of fallen bricks.

Up ahead Sherlock saw a length of tunnel that was bone dry. He grabbed the spoon from Watson. Jamming it down, he braked hard. The boat came to a stop right before ramming into the tunnel floor. "Cut the engines!" he cried.

Watson ran to the fan and switched it off.

Sherlock hopped out. "Help me carry the boat, quickly!" he commanded Watson. The two of them lifted the boat. They staggered down the tunnel until they came to an intersection where the water flowed again.

Sherlock and Watson jumped into the boat. Sherlock reached for the fan switch. He was just about to turn it on when Juliet and Gnomeo swooped in from a different tunnel. They blocked the path.

"Tell us what happened to our family!" Juliet demanded.

"We don't have time for this," Sherlock shouted. He picked up the spoon rudder and waved it at the two gnomes. "Now will you please step aside?"

Gnomeo gripped the edge of the boat and yanked down. "Not until you tell us what's going on around here."

Suddenly, a giant sewer rat emerged from the darkness. As it ran by, it nearly toppled the boat.

Sherlock shook his head in disgust. "Too late."

"What's too late?" Gnomeo asked.

Watson pointed down the tunnel. "Here they come."

Another rat rushed by. And then another. And another.

Sherlock glared at Gnomeo and Juliet. "And now we have a rat problem, thanks to these meddlesome amateurs."

Watson dropped to his hands and knees. He rummaged around the bottom of the boat until he pulled out a roll of dental floss. He unspooled a

long line of floss, and wrapped it around the hand-rail. Then he arched his back and flung the roll around a beam hanging from the top of the tunnel.

Tying off knots, Watson finished with his home-made pulley just as a giant stampede of rats started running directly toward them.

Sherlock held one end of the floss out to Gnomeo and Juliet. "If you don't want to get rat-trampled, I suggest you help Watson pull."

For a moment, Juliet and Gnomeo stood frozen with fear.

"Come on—give me a hand!" Watson yelled.

Juliet and Gnomeo sprang into action. Working together, they hauled away on the floss, lifting the boat up, inch by inch.

"Hurry!" Sherlock ordered. He sat at the back of the boat, looking displeased. Juliet, Gnomeo, and Watson barely managed to raise the boat out of the way before the rat stampede reached them.

It seemed to take forever for the chittering rodents to pass. Gnomeo looked over the side of the boat and immediately wished he hadn't. It would take just a single bite from one angry rat to lose a limb—or worse.

Once the stampede died down and the last rat was gone, Watson cut the floss and the boat plopped back down into the water.

Juliet slumped against the side of the boat. "Whew!" she gasped. "That was close." She felt her heartbeat slowly return back to normal.

"Whew?" snapped Sherlock. "What exactly do you think those rats were running *from*?"

A deep rumble echoed through the sewer. Gnomeo and Juliet stared at one another. Their eyes widened with fear. It seemed as though their nightmare was not yet over.

For a second, all was still.

And then a tidal wave of rushing water came flooding down the sewer tunnel.

Everyone hung on as the wave of stinky water slammed into them, hurling the boat through the sewer tunnels.

They hit a whirlpool and began to spin around faster and faster. Juliet saw Gnomeo lose his grip on the side of the boat. He slid helplessly back and forth, unable to grab on to anything.

The boat straightened and hurtled out of the whirlpool. Gnomeo managed to stand up just as a huge wave hit them. Juliet sprang into action.

"Gnomeo! No!" Juliet lunged forward and caught Gnomeo just as he was about to go flying out of the boat. With a mighty tug, she yanked him back to safety.

The stormy water finally started to subside and the waves flattened out. Gnomeo and Juliet sat and rested on the bottom of the boat. Watson clutched the spoon, looking green. Sherlock stood above him, calculating the probability that his partner would throw up. He was so busy staring at Watson that he didn't notice that the boat was headed straight toward a brick wall.

Upon impact, the bow disintegrated. Watson was thrown from the back of the boat and landed safely in the water. Gnomeo leaped off and grabbed on to the tunnel wall.

Juliet jumped onto the other side of the wall and turned her head. As she did, she saw Sherlock sailing by her, heading straight for the brick wall. She reached out and grabbed the detective by the edge of his coat just as the rest of the boat smashed to bits into the wall.

The water receded, leaving a sticky film of mud

behind it. Sherlock, Gnomeo, and Juliet carefully climbed down. As they cleaned themselves off, Gnomeo hugged Juliet. "Are you okay?" he asked.

Juliet didn't respond. She pulled away from Gnomeo and faced Sherlock, her hands on her hips. She had just saved Sherlock's life. "You were saying something about 'meddlesome amateurs'?" she asked sweetly.

Sherlock folded his arms. "I stand by that assessment. But if you insist on meddling, perhaps you could supplement Watson's efforts."

Watson sat up and spit out some sewer water. "How thoughtful," he muttered.

"What did you say your names were?" Sherlock asked.

"We didn't. I'm Gnomeo," said Gnomeo huffily.

"Juliet," said Juliet.

"I am Sherlock Gnomes, the world's first consulting detective and sworn protector of London's garden gnomes."

"And I am—" Watson began.

"To the surface!" Sherlock interrupted his partner. "We've not a moment to lose!"

As Sherlock headed down the tunnel, Juliet saw

the *M* card that had been left at her garden floating in the water. She picked it up and waved it in front of Watson. "Look, now that we're on the team, how about you tell us what's going on." She held the card up to Watson's nose. "Starting with this."

Watson nodded wearily. "Very well. The *M* stands for Moriarty—Sherlock's archenemy."

Chapter 11

As the gnomes headed to Chinatown through the sewer system, Watson filled Gnomeo and Juliet in on the details of Sherlock's most dangerous case. "Some ornaments are just manufactured evil," he began. "And Moriarty was the most evil of them all. No one comes close."

Sherlock turned a corner abruptly. The other gnomes bumped into one another and hastily changed direction to follow him.

"For years, Moriarty terrorized the ornamental world. Until he met his match in Sherlock Gnomes," Watson continued. He described how Moriarty loved to smash ornaments just for fun.

He had a pack of troll henchmen to help him. They often left a lot of evidence—broken pieces of porcelain and clay scattered throughout a garden. But never any witnesses.

"One day Sherlock came across Moriarty just as he was about to level a gnome garden with a bulldozer. Sherlock stopped him just in time, but he wasn't able to capture the evil villain.

"Moriarty escaped, but Sherlock had caught his eye," Watson said. He told Gnomeo and Juliet that Moriarty had been intrigued by Sherlock. He wanted to see just how powerful the detective's skills of deduction were.

"Moriarty began to play a terrible game. He would kidnap gnomes, leave a trail of clues as to their location, and challenge us to find them within twenty-four hours or he'd smash them." Watson shuddered, remembering the final time he and Sherlock had seen Moriarty. "We last battled him at the Natural History Museum. It was an encounter I'll never forget." He described how Moriarty had snuck into Hintze Hall with a sack full of gnomes, eager to smash them.

Watson and Sherlock had solved Moriarty's last

clue just a few minutes before their twenty-four hours were up. They had rushed to the museum and jimmied open a skylight. As they rappelled into Hintze Hall with Watson's grappling hooks, they saw Dippy, the giant diplodocus skeleton that had been the museum's main attraction for decades. They also saw a countdown clock on the wall with only twenty seconds left.

Dangling in midair, Sherlock had shouted, "Show yourself, Moriarty!"

Moriarty had stepped out of the shadows. "Sherlock! You're early again," he drawled. "How terribly rude. My henchmen have barely finished setting up. The goobarb pie filling has only just set."

Sherlock and Watson saw dozens of gnomes plastered onto a large barrel suspended from the ceiling. They were held in place by a sticky jam filling.

Moriarty grabbed a rolling pin and leaped onto Dippy's tail. He scurried up the dinosaur's spine until he was within striking distance of the detective. "Come, Sherlock, come dance with me!" he crowed as he swung at Sherlock with the pin.

Watson reached down and grabbed a loose dinosaur bone. He tossed it to Sherlock.

Sherlock unhitched himself from the grappling rope and landed next to Moriarty. The dinosaur swayed and they both wobbled, nearly losing their balance.

Sherlock was the first to regain his footing. *"En garde!"* he cried.

Moriarty frowned. "I wanted to say that!" He steadied himself and attacked Sherlock anew.

As Sherlock fought with Moriarty on the dinosaur skeleton, Watson had rappelled down to the ground. He peered up. The gnomes were struggling to free themselves from the sticky goobarb, but even if they had, they would have plunged to the hard tile floor below.

Watson looked around him. He saw glass display cases and a neatly swept floor. Then he saw a janitor's cart against the far wall. It had a mop, a bucket, window-washing liquid, and a huge bottle of soap.

Overhead, Moriarty had jabbed at Sherlock with his rolling pin. "Be honest, Sherlock," he cooed. "You enjoy our little game as much as I do."

"This is no game, Moriarty!" Sherlock ducked under the pin, and parried. "I am the sworn protector of London's garden gnomes!"

Watson got an idea. As the countdown timer ticked on, he ran over to the janitor's cart. He pushed it forward with all his strength, knocking away the troll henchmen like pins in a bowling alley.

He ran to the other side of the cart, and managed to stop it right below the suspended barrel. Grabbing the soap bottle, he leaped onto the barrel and dumped soap over the sides.

One by one, the gnomes worked themselves free of the sticky goobarb and dropped safely onto the cart. As the last gnome peeled himself off the barrel, Watson jumped onto the ground. He heaved the cart out of the way just as the timer hit zero. The barrel dropped to the ground. Narrowly missing the cart, it had hit the floor and splintered into pieces.

At the same time, Sherlock had finally knocked the rolling pin out of Moriarty's hand. The villain leaped from the dinosaur onto a power cord dangling from the wall. "If you are the sworn protector of the city's gnomes, then I am their sworn destroyer!" he cackled. "And we will keep playing this little game, Sherlock, until I crush every last gnome in London."

As he spoke, the power cord plug came out of the outlet.

"Oh fudge," Moriarty groaned. He fell, bounced off the scaffolding, and landed on the floor, still intact.

Dippy started to teeter. Sherlock lost his balance and nearly fell off.

"Sherlock!" Watson shouted. He vaulted himself onto the scaffolding. Just before Sherlock plummeted to the ground, Watson fired a grappling hook from his cane. Sherlock caught it, and Watson swung him to safety.

Moriarty looked up. "Double fudge," he had muttered as the entire dinosaur skeleton collapsed into a dusty pile of rubble on top of him.

"Sherlock! Our hero!" the gnomes cheered.

Sherlock brushed himself off and turned to his partner. "Watson!"

Watson looked up hopefully.

Sherlock tossed the cane back to him. "Yours, I believe," he said curtly before inspecting the wreckage in the front lobby.

All that had been left of Moriarty was his hat.

"We thought that was the last of Moriarty, but

we were wrong. He's back," Watson finished. He flipped over the *M* card to reveal an 8:43 time stamp. "And unless we find the kidnapped gnomes within twenty-four hours, Moriarty is going to smash them all."

"He's going to smash our friends and family?" said Gnomeo incredulously.

"How do we stop him?" asked Juliet.

"We play his game," answered Sherlock. "We follow his trail of clues and find the gnomes before 8:43 p.m. tomorrow night." He beckoned to the others and pointed to a metal ladder that led up to a manhole cover. "We have arrived," he said. He began to climb.

Watson, Gnomeo, and Juliet followed.

Chapter 12

On a dark, deserted street, a manhole cover slid aside. Four gnomes climbed out of the sewer and looked around. A painted metal gate with a green roof tipped with fire-breathing dragons rose above them. Strings of Chinese and British flags criss-crossed the redbrick row houses that lined the street. They had arrived in Chinatown.

Sherlock darted down an empty alley and sprang up onto a Dumpster. He beckoned for the gnomes to follow him through an open window.

The gnomes hopped through the window and found themselves in a cluttered shop. Every last inch of every last shelf was filled with knickknacks and gifts.

"Where are we?" whispered Gnomeo.

"Curly Fu's Chinese Emporium," Sherlock replied. "Let's go around the back."

The gnomes leaped onto a shelf and crawled behind a row of brightly colored vases. They snuck past a young man listening to his headphones and arrived at the clothing section of the store.

"If you recall, the last time we were here, it was a bit of a catastrophe," Watson reminded Sherlock.

Sherlock frowned. "Yes, I have a faint memory of some unpleasantness." He leaped onto a box and tossed clothes and accessories down to Gnomeo and Juliet. "I need to find the next clue. Put these disguises on so we don't get spotted."

Once everyone was in costume, the gnomes hurried to the end of the store. Juliet pushed back a beaded curtain to find a bustling area filled with different Chinese ornaments.

"Now, just act natural," instructed Sherlock.

As the gnomes walked down the aisles, a Chinese ornament spotted them and rushed off. A gong sounded.

All of a sudden, dozens of lucky cats appeared around the corner. They led an elaborate procession

and marched in an elegant line right toward the gnomes.

"I'm fairly sure we've been spotted," Watson told Sherlock.

Tiny white lucky cats rounded the corner, carrying an enormous golden lucky cat on a pillow. Sherlock and Watson bowed and batted the air.

A saltshaker figurine emerged to translate. "Her Highness the Grand Empress Dowager Pom-Pom," he announced.

"Meow," said the giant golden lucky cat.

"Empress Pom-Pom remembers you, Sherlock Gnomes," intoned the saltshaker.

"Oh good!" exclaimed Sherlock.

"Not fondly," the saltshaker said.

"Ah," said Sherlock. He shrank down in his coat a little. "Less good."

Watson cleared his throat. "I see you got the orchid I sent to apologize for our last encounter?"

"Meow," said Empress Pom-Pom.

"A gracious gift," the saltshaker translated. "But you are not the one who offended the empress. Sherlock is. As such, I'm afraid I must ask you all to leave."

"He's very sorry," said Watson. He turned to Sherlock. "Tell her how sorry you are."

"I'm sorry I wasted my time solving your case," said Sherlock.

Watson bowed low to the empress. "Now, technically that was an apology."

"Dozens of gnomes are in danger, so would you kindly step aside and let me continue my investigation?" said Sherlock.

"Meow. Meow, meow, meow. Meow . . . meow, meow," said Empress Pom-Pom.

"No," said the saltshaker.

Empress Pom-Pom signaled and two red lucky cats appeared. They were big and muscular and looked very much like bodyguards. They motioned for the gnomes to leave.

Juliet stepped forward. "Please, we just need to take a look around," she pleaded. "It's very important."

The two red lucky cats advanced on Juliet.

"Wait, wait, wait, let me explain," said Juliet.

The cats continued to advance.

Gnomeo jumped in front of Juliet. "Oi! I'm warning you. Back off!" he cried. As the cats

leaped, Gnomeo knocked both of them aside.

One of the red lucky cats tumbled down the aisle. The other one crashed headlong into a tiny white cat.

The tiny white cat staggered and meowed loudly. The pillow wobbled ever so slightly. Then the tiny white cat bumped into another tiny white cat. Like dominoes, all the cats holding Empress Pom-Pom's pillow toppled over. The empress went flying.

"Screech!" yelled Empress Pom-Pom.

"Guards!" called the saltshaker.

The lucky cats helped the empress to her feet and then wheeled on Juliet and Gnomeo. They hissed menacingly.

Sherlock turned to the other gnomes. "You have to fend them off, so I can find the clue."

"Ah, here we go again," sighed Watson.

"You help Watson," Juliet told Gnomeo. "I'll help Sherlock." She ran down the aisle after Sherlock.

"Huh? Oh great," groaned Gnomeo. He turned to one of the lucky cats and raised his fists. "All right. Me and you, let's have it."

Chapter 13

As Gnomeo and Watson battled the lucky cats, Sherlock and Juliet raced through the aisles. Sherlock's eyes darted back and forth.

"What are we looking for?" shouted Juliet.

"I'm currently looking for a moment of silence so I can concentrate," Sherlock said. He glared at Juliet, and for a moment she wondered if she should have stayed back to help Gnomeo and Watson.

Suddenly, Sherlock stopped short. He scanned the emporium with his Sherlock vision. He was sure Moriarty had left some kind of clue. He just had to find it.

As he gazed along the shelves, his hypersensitive

vision zoomed onto one object. He pointed. "Up there!" he said. He climbed to the topmost shelf and showed Juliet what had caught his eye. It was a cuckoo clock.

Sherlock turned the clock over in his hands. "This shouldn't be here," he said. "A clock is a terribly offensive gift in Chinese culture." On a hunch, he brought the clock hands to 8:43.

The doors of the clock sprang open. But instead of a cuckoo bird, a model airplane flew out. On one wing, a red, white, blue, and yellow circle had been painted next to the letters *N* and *V*. An *M* card was stuck to its other wing.

"A plane? Is that a clue?" asked Juliet.

Sherlock removed the card. The clock started to cuckoo.

"Uh, oh." Juliet looked down to see a pack of lucky cats running down the aisle. Sherlock tried to jam the clock doors shut, but it was too late. The cats spotted the two gnomes. They crouched low, tails lashing, and pounced.

Juliet grabbed a pair of chopsticks from the shelf. She threw one to Sherlock and brandished the other one herself. As the clock cuckooed loudly, they jabbed at the lucky cats, fending off the first wave of attacking felines. But down the aisle, more were heading their way.

"Juliet, we're coming!" shouted a familiar voice. It was Gnomeo, closely followed by Watson. They sprinted down the aisle and leaped onto the shelf, knocking off the lucky cats that had managed to land there.

Sherlock dropped his chopstick and held up the *M* card, studying it. "Curious, a different pattern," he mused. His brain cells whizzed about, making connections. He nodded to himself, and then tossed the card away. "Let's go!" he commanded.

The gnomes climbed down from the shelf just as a new wave of lucky cats hurtled toward them. They wove through the aisles, searching for a way out. As they ran, Sherlock scanned the shelves. He saw paper lanterns and store signs with suction cups on them. He spotted a high window. "This way!" he called.

As the gnomes ran to the window, Sherlock grabbed the paper lanterns and suction cups off the shelf. He threw them toward the others. "This might work," he said.

The gnomes followed Sherlock up and out of the window. Sherlock slammed the window shut behind them. "This way! Hurry up!" he shouted.

The lucky cats started to claw open the window. They were still coming!

"That steam pipe across the street," Sherlock told Watson.

Watson knew exactly what to do. He pressed a button on his cane, and the bottom of it opened. A grappling hook attached to a line of string tumbled out.

Watson sunk the grappling hook into the windowsill. When he was sure it was firmly anchored, he hurled his cane. The crook of the cane caught neatly onto the steam pipe of the building next door.

"Wow! Nice!" said Gnomeo.

Sherlock handed everyone a paper lantern. "Put these on. Follow me. Quickly now." He donned a lantern and began to crawl across the string. Watson, Juliet, and then Gnomeo followed. From below, they looked just like another string of lanterns in Chinatown.

Sherlock reached the steam pipe first. He

climbed up, already heading for the roof. Behind them, the horde of yowling lucky cats had managed to open the window.

Watson was the next gnome to make it to safety. He reached the pipe just as an enormous lucky cat with an evil smile on her face appeared at the window. As Juliet jumped onto the pipe, a single claw sprang out from the cat's paw.

Sherlock looked down. "You may want to go faster," he told Gnomeo as the lucky cat leaned out and began to saw away at the grappling hook string.

"Yeah, yeah, yeah. Thanks for the tip," muttered Gnomeo.

The string broke just as Gnomeo reached the pipe. He nearly fell, but just managed to pull himself to safety. "Meow this!" he cried to the hissing cats at the window. He brought his hand up and batted it down, doing a mocking lucky cat salute.

"Come on! And bring your lanterns!" cried Sherlock. He had made it to the rooftop. Watson and Juliet were not far behind.

Gnomeo scowled, got to his feet, and then followed.

Chapter 14

Sherlock rushed across the rooftops of Chinatown. He did not look back to see if the other gnomes were keeping up. Luckily, they were. After they had raced across the entire neighborhood, Sherlock came to a stop on a ledge.

The detective held a finger up in the air, calculating the wind. "Get ready with those suction cups," he ordered. He attached the suction cups to his feet, and the other gnomes did the same. "On my mark," he said.

"Wait, what are we doing?" asked Juliet.

Sherlock sighed in exasperation. He thought it had been obvious. "Jumping, of course." He stepped off the roof.

Juliet gasped and ran to the ledge. Holding her breath, she looked down.

Sherlock was floating calmly down toward the street. He held the lantern over his head and was using it as a parachute.

Juliet closed her eyes. Then she took a deep breath and leaped.

"No!" Gnomeo couldn't believe that Juliet had jumped. He turned to Watson, about to ask if there was another way down. But Sherlock's partner was already on the ledge. Before Gnomeo could say a word, Watson was gone.

Gnomeo gritted his teeth. He double-checked his lantern to make sure there weren't any rips in it. Then he held his breath and jumped off the ledge.

The gnomes sailed through the air, held up by their lantern parachutes. Frightened pigeons squawked and got out of their way. A few humans saw the gnomes, but figured it was just a few stray paper lanterns floating in the breeze.

Since he had taken so long to jump, Gnomeo was a few yards behind the others. He saw them land on top of a red double-decker bus. He yanked on his lantern and guided himself toward the bus.

But just before Gnomeo landed, the bus veered right and changed lanes. Gnomeo barely managed to catch the edge of the back of the bus as he landed.

"Suction cups down!" ordered Sherlock. He had landed at the front of the bus, while Gnomeo, Juliet, and Watson were toward the rear.

The gnomes stomped down on the suction cups, and stuck themselves to the bus. Once he was steady, Gnomeo turned to help Juliet. But she was already scooting her way up toward Sherlock, leaving him behind.

Juliet crouched down next to Sherlock. "The plane. Are we going to an airport or something?" she asked.

"Juliet!" Gnomeo called.

Juliet didn't respond. She was too busy waiting for Sherlock's answer.

Sherlock shook his head. "Moriarty's clues are never quite that simple."

Gnomeo watched Juliet talking to Sherlock. She was completely ignoring him. He got angrier and angrier. After all they had been through, he was losing her to some slick detective with a goofy hat!

Gnomeo was so mad, he lost track of the fact that he was whizzing at high speed on top of a bus. Suddenly, the bus turned a corner and his suction cups peeled off. He slid across the slippery metal roof, desperately trying to grab on to something. But there was nothing to grab.

Gnomeo skittered to the edge of the bus. Just as he flew off, a hand reached out and grabbed him.

Only instead of it being Juliet who saved him, it was Watson. "Hang on!" he cried. He leaned back against the wind, and barely managed to wrestle Gnomeo back onto the bus. "You okay?" he asked.

Gnomeo shrugged, pretending that he hadn't been terrified at all. "Cheers, mate," he said. He looked over to see if Juliet had been worried about him.

Juliet was huddled with Sherlock at the front of the bus. Her back was turned to Gnomeo. She hadn't even known that he had nearly gotten smashed to bits.

"Are you sure you can find them?" Juliet asked Sherlock.

"Rest assured, I will crack this clue. I will find your friends and family. I've never failed to solve

80

a case, and I don't plan on starting now," Sherlock said.

An hour later, the double-decker bus turned onto a wide avenue lined with London plane trees and a long wrought iron gate. As it rumbled down a street, four gnomes, two at the front of the bus, and two at the back, peered out from the roof.

"We'll have to jump onto that tree," Sherlock told Juliet. He pointed to a large plane tree halfway down the block.

Juliet turned to Gnomeo and Watson. "Get ready to jump."

Gnomeo rolled his eyes. "Yeah, sure, whatever you say." He had just about had it with taking orders.

As they passed the tree, Sherlock quickly shouted, "Jump!"

The gnomes leaped onto a low-hanging branch. As the bus drove off, they made their way to the trunk and quickly hid among the leaves.

Unlike the Chinatown alleyways where no one was around, the street below them buzzed with activity. Humans walked about, talking and texting, or listening silently to the music streaming into their headphones. A stream of cars drove by, honking politely at one another. It was not a safe place for a gnome to be out in the open.

Watson pointed across the street. Gnomeo and Juliet looked to see an elegant terra-cotta building with twin towers and a cathedral entrance in front of them. They had arrived at the Natural History Museum.

"The site of our last showdown with Moriarty," Watson whispered. "Of course! That's where the clue is leading us."

"Moriarty would never choose such an obvious location," Sherlock scoffed.

Watson shrank down against his cane, looking hurt.

Gnomeo glared at Sherlock. "All right, smart guy," he growled. "What's *your* plan?"

"If you must know, we are going to the DeJong exhibit at the art gallery. I haven't cracked the latest clue yet, and the art helps me ruminate." Sherlock pointed far down the street to the gallery. It was three blocks away.

Gnomeo couldn't believe it. "*That's* your plan?" he cried. "Art and thinking? Your museum's right there! Let's just go check it out."

Sherlock didn't respond.

"Mate, think about it," continued Gnomeo. "You beat this guy at the museum, right? And now he wants revenge. Don't you get it? He's waiting for you at the museum. He wants a rematch!"

Sherlock wasn't paying the slightest attention to Gnomeo. His eyes glazed over as he went deep into his mind palace.

"Plus, we can get in right there." Gnomeo pointed to an entrance. He looked at Sherlock. "Are you . . . are you . . . is he even listening to me?" He turned to the others and waved a hand in front of Sherlock's face. The detective did not respond. "He's not listening, look!" Gnomeo cried. He dropped his hand, defeated.

Sherlock sighed with relief. "Oh good. You stopped talking. Now we can go to the gallery."

Gnomeo was fed up. "You know what, good luck with that. We're going to the museum." He reached for Juliet, but she didn't take his hand.

"Let's just go to the gallery," she told Gnomeo.

"Are you serious? You're seriously choosing him over me?" Gnomeo cried.

Juliet folded her arms. "I'm not choosing anyone. Sherlock knows this Moriarty guy and you don't."

"We're supposed to be partners. Gnomeo and Juliet, remember?" said Gnomeo.

"We *are* partners," insisted Juliet.

"Well, it doesn't feel like it. It hasn't felt like it since we moved here," said Gnomeo.

Juliet didn't know how to answer. Gnomeo was her true love, but she needed to save her friends and family. She needed to put the garden first. And Sherlock seemed like the only gnome who could help her.

Gnomeo reached for Juliet's hand again. "Are you with me or not?"

Juliet shook her head and pulled away. "Don't do this."

There was a long silence.

"And there it is," said Gnomeo heavily. He dropped his hand and shimmied down the tree by himself. Ducking through the grass, he ran toward the museum.

"Good," said Sherlock. "Now we can go to the gallery."

"Should we go after him?" asked Watson.

"No, *we* shouldn't. But *you* may waste your time if you want." Sherlock climbed down to the ground. With brisk, decisive steps, he headed toward the modern art gallery.

"Sherlock Gnomes." Watson sighed. He turned to Juliet. "Don't worry. I'll get Gnomeo back."

Chapter 15

It was warm and silent in the Natural History Museum. Slipping through an open window, Watson crept past the guards and made his way into Hintze Hall. Dippy the dinosaur was no longer there. A gigantic blue whale skeleton suspended from the ceiling had taken his place. The whale glowed under an eerie blue light in the empty hall. "Gnomeo? Gnomeo?" called Watson. He groaned. "Oh, don't make me say it. Wherefore art thou, Gnomeo?"

"You all right, mate?" a voice asked. It was directly behind Watson.

Watson yelped and whirled around. "Cheese and crackers!"

"Sorry for scaring you." Gnomeo peered hopefully behind Watson, trying to see if Juliet was there too.

She wasn't.

"It's just you, then?" Gnomeo said, disappointed.

Watson nodded. "We were hoping you'd join us at the gallery."

Gnomeo folded his arms angrily. "Not gonna happen, mate. I'm sure we were right about the museum, and I'm going to prove it." He took off running.

Watson sighed. He looked at the skeleton of a velociraptor displayed along the side of the hall. It seemed to be smirking at him. "Oh, don't look at me like that," he told the dinosaur. "I'm trying my best." He went after Gnomeo.

Gnomeo tore past glass cases filled with fossils, sea creature displays, a butterfly garden, and countless wildlife exhibits, looking for any clue that would prove that he had been right. He wanted to show Juliet that she had been wrong to abandon him. To doubt him. To think that Sherlock was better than her own partner.

"Look, I know you're angry," said Watson as he struggled to keep up with Gnomeo.

"How would you feel?" cried Gnomeo. He raced angrily through another hallway. "It's like she doesn't even care about me."

"A partner who takes you for granted?" Watson grinned wryly. "I can't think of what that's like."

Gnomeo stopped. He turned to Watson and shook his head. "I don't know how you put up with that gnome."

"And if we had six months, I'd list all his faults, but despite them he is a brilliant detective . . ."

Gnomeo held up his hand. Watson's voice trailed off as they heard the sound of flapping wings approaching them. Whatever was flying down the hallway was very, very big.

"What is that?" cried Gnomeo as the sound drew closer and the shadow grew larger.

A stone gargoyle landed in front of them. Her razor-sharp claws dug into the floor, leaving rake marks on the tile. Her pointed ears were drawn back as she opened her mouth, revealing a ghastly row of teeth.

"Boo," said the gargoyle. "If I were you I'd run."

Gnomeo and Watson didn't need to be asked twice. They bolted down the hallway with the gargoyle in

hot pursuit. As they sprinted, Watson spotted an open skylight window. "Up there!" he cried.

Just as he spoke, he tripped and went skidding across the floor. His cane flew out of his hands. The gargoyle loomed over the fallen gnome. She chuckled as she reached out for Watson with her claws.

Suddenly, Watson's cane went sailing through the air. It smashed right into the gargoyle's nose. "Oi! Ugly, over here!" Gnomeo shouted. He had hurled the cane at the beast, and had hit his mark.

The gargoyle growled and took off after Gnomeo.

"Go!" Gnomeo yelled to Watson. He reached some scaffolding and began to climb.

"Not so fast," the gargoyle said. She grabbed ahold of Gnomeo. "Got ya!"

Gnomeo looked up at the leering face. He gulped. "Do you know that up close you're actually quite handsome—whoa!" he yelled as the gargoyle picked him up and flew off.

Meanwhile Sherlock and Juliet were hopping from tree to tree, keeping in the shadows on the way to the modern art gallery.

As they neared their destination, for the tenth time, Juliet stole a glance back at the Natural History Museum.

"Why do you keep looking back?" asked Sherlock. "He just severed your partnership!"

"We didn't break up," whispered Juliet. "It was just a fight."

"Hmmmmm," said Sherlock. He started to climb down a tree.

"Hey, what do you mean—" Juliet began, but Sherlock had already slid out of sight and earshot. She slid down the tree and found Sherlock pressed against the base of the trunk. "What exactly does 'hmmmmm' mean?" she asked.

Sherlock peeked around the corner of the tree, and then jerked back. A group of tourists was walking down the sidewalk. The coast was definitely not clear. "It means you were young and in love but your new garden duties were too much for a young couple to handle. Likelihood of a breakup: ninety-nine percent." Sherlock noticed Juliet's glare. "I rounded down."

As Juliet looked again toward the museum, an enormous shadow cut across the night sky. "Did you see that?" she gasped.

Shrouded in fog, the shadow flew directly into the museum.

Juliet began to run back toward the museum, but Sherlock grabbed her and pulled her back. Holding his finger up to his lips, he motioned toward the other side of the tree. Juliet saw a maintenance man heading toward them.

Sherlock motioned for Juliet to follow him, and they ducked for cover under the bushes. Being careful not be to seen, they ran from bush to bush, heading back toward the Natural History Museum.

They finally arrived, just in time to see Watson perched precariously on the edge of a skylight window. As he wobbled, trying to keep his balance, a gargoyle stepped out of the window. She had a familiar figure in her talons.

"Gnomeo!" Juliet covered her mouth in horror as the beast unfurled its wings and flew off, carrying her partner away. As it did, it knocked Watson off the window.

Juliet and Sherlock watched helplessly as Watson tumbled through the air and out of sight. A few seconds later, they heard the horrible sound of something smashing into the ground.

Sherlock bowed his head. "Watson," he pronounced solemnly.

"No!" cried Juliet.

"Come along, Miss Juliet. We must keep going," said Sherlock.

Chapter 16

Juliet trailed after Sherlock as he headed down the block. When they reached the DeJong exhibit at the art gallery, Sherlock pulled open a grate and they made their way inside.

"The museum was clearly a trap," said Sherlock. "And the gargoyle explains the absence of footprints. Remind me to retrieve Watson's map of gnomes as soon as I've resolved this case."

"The map!" Juliet snapped. "That's what you care about? The map?"

"It's one-of-a-kind," said Sherlock. "And in the wrong hands—"

"Watson just got smashed!" cried Juliet. "Aren't

you at all sad or angry about your friend?"

"Sadness and anger won't help me save your friends and family. Nor will it bring Watson back to life." Sherlock looked at Juliet hard. "I've already failed one gnome tonight. I will not fail another."

"Fine," retorted Juliet. "What do we do now?"

"I will crack this clue. And *you* will stand over there and be very quiet," said Sherlock.

"Let me help you!" pleaded Juliet.

"It would take far too long to explain all the variables," Sherlock said, irritated.

Juliet tried one last time. "But just give me something—"

"My deduction can't wait!" shouted Sherlock. He gave Juliet a cold gaze. "You *can*."

Juliet felt like she had been stabbed in the heart. She had heard those words before. She had said them to Gnomeo. And now, she wasn't sure she would ever be able to take them back.

"I'll let you know when I've cracked the clue," continued Sherlock briskly. He walked over to a Styrofoam sculpture and froze in meditation.

Juliet waved her hand in front of the detective's face.

Sherlock was gone.

Juliet slumped on the cold hard floor of the museum. Before long, she was asleep.

As early morning light flooded through the museum, Juliet woke to Sherlock shaking her shoulder. "I have it!" he announced.

Juliet rubbed her eyes and got to her feet. As they headed toward the museum exit, Sherlock explained his theory. "The circle on the plane is a symbol used by the *Royal* Air Force," he said. "So, the clue involves something *royal*. The plane also bore the letters *N-V*. Two letters, but also a word. "Envy." As in *green* with envy. And thus we have two pieces of the puzzle: *royal* and *green*."

The sound of the museum's cleaning crew echoed through the hallway. Sherlock and Juliet ducked into a side room, narrowly avoiding discovery.

"But I remained vexed," continued Sherlock. "Why a plane? And then it struck me. The planatus tree, also known as the *plane* tree, is the most common tree . . . in *Royal Green* Park!"

The sound of the cleaners faded away, and Sherlock and Juliet made their way to the exit. "Come along, Miss Juliet," said Sherlock. "It's already nine a.m., and we have less than twelve hours to save those gnomes."

"How are we supposed to get around a public park in broad daylight?" asked Juliet.

"Ah, fear not," said Sherlock. "For I am not just a master of deduction—I am also a master of disguise."

At Royal Green Park, a maintenance worker drove a riding mower across the grass. He passed by a few joggers, the occasional dog walker, and a staggering squirrel.

The squirrel ran left. Then right. Then right. Then right again. Inside, Sherlock was in the front of the squirrel costume, and Juliet was holding up the rear.

"Come on. Let's go," hissed Sherlock. "Two forward. Hold. Three forward. Hold. I said *hold*!" he groaned as Juliet bumped into him for the twentieth time. He sighed. "Tell me, does our squirrel have some sort of rabies-induced illness, or did he have too much to drink?"

"Oh, forgive me," said Juliet sarcastically. "I've never been the back end of a squirrel before!"

"You should have told me that before I took you on as my assistant," huffed Sherlock.

Juliet stopped. "I'm not your—"

"Shh! We've been spotted," warned Sherlock.

Other squirrels in the park looked in their direction.

"Wiggle your rear end," Sherlock instructed.

"What?" Juliet stammered.

"Quickly!" Sherlock whispered urgently. Go on! Wiggle!"

"Fine." Juliet made a face and shook her bottom.

Sherlock looked around to see how she was doing. "A real squirrel would greet the other squirrels by wagging its tail. Now please just shake your bottom harder."

Juliet shuddered. "Ugh, and feminism takes a step backward." She wiggled harder.

"That is the least realistic tail wagging I've ever seen," Sherlock said. But Juliet's squirrel imitation had worked. The other squirrels went back to chasing each other up trees and hunting for nuts.

Sherlock and Juliet stopped in the middle of the

park. As birds sang and tweeted around them, they scanned the area for clues. All they saw were endless rows of trees.

Juliet groaned. "There are hundreds of plane trees. The clue could be anywhere."

"Shhh!" Sherlock put a finger to his lips. "I'm trying to listen. Do you hear that?" He concentrated. "The chirping sound. That's no birdcall. It's Morse code for the letter *M*." He listened more closely. "Good grief, don't move," he hissed.

Juliet peeked out from under the costume and saw a dog snoring nearby. "It's just a dog," she said, exasperated.

"Just a dog?" Sherlock was inflamed. "I know the identity of seven hundred and eighty-four dogs in this city. And in this very park, that very dog bit me. I'll never forget it."

"I'm siding with the dog here," Juliet said.

"First Chinatown, now Toby, both unpleasant past encounters," Sherlock mused. "This is no coincidence. Toby must have our next clue."

The two gnomes carefully walked toward the sleeping dog. Sherlock spied a toy bone under its paws. He motioned for Juliet to grab it.

Juliet reached out from under the squirrel costume. Working gently, she managed to pry the bone from Toby's paws.

"Now, quietly, look for a clue," Sherlock said.

Juliet saw something hidden inside the bone. She reached in and dug it out.

"But whatever you do, don't—" Sherlock began.

The toy bone squeaked.

"Oh dear," Sherlock said.

Toby woke up and started to growl. He began to stalk Sherlock and Juliet.

Sherlock backed up. "This way," he said.

In the distance, Juliet saw something that would help them escape. "No, *this* way," she told Sherlock. She pointed to the mower, and the two gnomes started running toward it. When they reached it, Sherlock started up the engine as Juliet took the steering wheel. Toby was nearly upon them.

"Head for those laurel bushes," Sherlock yelled.

"Give him the bone!" Juliet yelled back.

Sherlock took the bone and threw it. Toby jumped up and missed it.

Sherlock gunned the mower. Dodging the trees and pedestrians, Juliet expertly steered them to the edge of the park. They leaped off and hid behind a trash bin. Sherlock took off his half of the squirrel costume. "Well, that was an unconventional bit of parking," he said as Juliet wriggled out of the squirrel suit. "Miss Juliet, I should tell you something."

Juliet smiled at Sherlock. She was sure he was about to thank her for their quick escape.

"That is not how a squirrel shakes its behind. This is." Sherlock shook his bottom in front of Juliet. "Do you see what I'm doing? Do you see? Do you see?"

"Yes, you're acting like a rear end." Juliet sighed. "Can we check out the clue?" She held up a button with an *M* on it.

Sherlock paled. "Of course this would be next. Moriarty, you monster," he muttered. "Forcing me to face my greatest fears."

Juliet snorted. "A button. Really?"

"This button is far less innocent than it appears. Oh, this is low, even for Moriarty." Sherlock steeled himself. "Very well. If he wants to dance, then dance we shall!"

Chapter 17

In another part of London, a bleary-eyed stone gargoyle awoke from his sleep to the sound of banging on the front door. Yawning, he shuffled through an elegant room with a huge fireplace, decorated with gold trim and Victorian furniture. He opened the door.

A hulking gargoyle handed him a squirming sack. "This one's a handful, Reggie," she said.

"Why do I have to babysit and you get to do the fun stuff?" Reggie whined. "It's not fair, Ronnie."

Ronnie shrugged. "Boss likes me better than you." She spread her wings and took off as Reggie brought the sack into the room. He tossed the sack on the floor, and Gnomeo burst out.

"Lemme out, you big—" Gnomeo stopped. He couldn't believe his eyes. In front of him were hundreds of gnomes. They were milling about, playing with items from an old cardboard box marked LOST PROPERTY. And in the corner, he spotted a familiar blue cap.

"Gnomeo!" Lady Bluebury saw Gnomeo. She rushed over to her son and wrapped him up in a gigantic hug. "Oh thank goodness," she said happily. "Did those awful monsters hurt you?"

"I'm fine, Ma," said Gnomeo. In seconds, he was mobbed by all his friends and family from the garden.

"Juliet's not with you. Where is she? Is she okay?" asked Lord Redbrick.

"She's fine," said Gnomeo. "She—"

"She dumped you," said Nanette. She sighed. "I knew it. I don't know why you thought you could fix things with a grand romantic gesture. That is just dumb. Talk about pulling a Gnomeo."

"We didn't . . ." Gnomeo frowned. "Wait, 'pulling a Gnomeo' means doing something cool."

Nanette rolled her eyes. "Oh yeah. Right. That's totally how we all use that phrase."

"What's going on here?" Gnomeo asked.

Fawn pointed a hoof at the gargoyle. "So, you know how gnomes were being abducted? Well, it turns out that the gargoyles had heard that something big was going down tonight with all of London's gnomes. They were worried, so they brought all the gnomes here for safekeeping. That was nice of them."

"They're gonna take us home after tonight," said Mankini.

"Yeah," Paris chimed in. "They even promised us a big surprise. He brought his hands together and swooped them up like they were shooting stars, then fluttered them down like bits of ash and dust. "And they did *that* when they said it, which I thought seemed a bit ominous, like we weren't going to get a big surprise, or if we do it's going to be something really unspeakably horrific. But it might just be balloons."

Gnomeo shared a worried look with Lady Bluebury and Lord Redbrick. "That's great, guys. Go have fun," he told them.

As the other ornaments ran off, Gnomeo huddled together with his mother and Juliet's father. "We're in trouble. Big trouble," he said.

Lady Bluebury nodded. "We know, dear. We didn't want to worry the others."

"How bad is it?" asked Lord Redbrick.

"This Moriarty guy, he's going to smash us all tonight," Gnomeo whispered.

Across the room, a tiny gnome perked up his giant ears. "We're going to be smashed?" he yelled. "This guy said we're all going to be smashed tonight."

Fawn looked disappointed. "Well, that's not a very good surprise."

As the other gnomes started to scream, Reggie banged his fist on the floor. "Quiet down, now!" he ordered. He drummed his claws on the floorboards menacingly.

Gnomeo huddled around his friends and family. "There must be a way out of here," he said in a hushed tone.

Lady Bluebury pointed toward the ceiling. "The only way out is through that skylight."

Gnomeo looked around thoughtfully. "But it's so high. What about the door? Has anyone tried barging through it?"

Benny gestured to a gnome who was holding his arm. It had been smashed off at the shoulder. "Yeah, that guy."

"Skylight it is," Gnomeo said. He looked around the room. "Benny, do you think that if I use those trowels as climbing gear I could scale those bricks on the fireplace and use the goons to swing to the beam? Then I could tightrope walk across it, we could reach the skylight, get around the door, and open it from the other side, leading everyone to victory." He turned around.

Benny had vanished.

"Benny!" Gnomeo whispered. A hand tapped him on the shoulder. He whirled around.

"If you're going to escape, we'll need to create a distraction," Lord Redbrick said. He pointed to Benny, who had fallen out of the lost property box.

Benny staggered to his feet. He was wearing a pink frilly scarf. It billowed around him.

Reggie saw Benny and chuckled. "Ha, ha. Looks like a princess, a girl."

The gnomes shared a look.

Lady Bluebury winked at Gnomeo. "I believe we just found our distraction."

Chapter 18

On the crowded streets of central London, Sherlock mimicked the sound of a "text received" whistle. Everyone stopped to check their phone, allowing him and Juliet to pass by unnoticed.

Using Sherlock's text whistle, the two gnomes had been able to travel in broad daylight along the London streets. They had made it to an above-ground subway station, and watched as a train sped by, clattering along the tracks.

"Is that the underground?" Juliet whispered. "I thought that it was, well, underground."

"Despite its name, nearly fifty-eight percent of the underground is actually aboveground," Sherlock explained. "Humans use it to travel around London. Now, would you like to see Big Ben, or can we get on with our investigation?"

He whistled and strode across the street. Juliet bit back an angry reply and followed.

They stopped in front of a brightly painted building. Its window display was made entirely of toys. "There it is," Sherlock whispered. "He pointed to a sign that read DOYLE'S DOLL MUSEUM.

"The Doll Museum?" Juliet said.

Sherlock nodded gravely. "The Doll Museum. I must now confront the most terrifying ornament in all of London."

"Moriarty?" Juliet guessed.

Sherlock corrected himself. "I must now confront the *second* most terrifying ornament in all of London." Motioning for Juliet to follow, he snuck around to a tiny door at the back of the museum. He rapped twice, paused, rapped five more times, and coughed.

A miniature eye slot opened. "You sure you wanna come in here?" asked someone with a high-pitched voice.

Sherlock nodded.

The door opened, revealing a giant teddy bear holding a much smaller teddy bear.

"Your funeral," cackled the smaller bear. The larger bear silently led Sherlock and Juliet inside.

They passed dozens of empty display cases until they arrived at a makeshift arena in the middle of a room. Hundreds of different dolls were piled on stadium seats, cheering on an enormous gorilla. The gorilla was beating his chest.

Juliet turned to Sherlock. "Yikes. The second most terrifying ornament, I presume."

Sherlock shook his head. "Not him."

A giant robot entered, waving its enormous steel arms.

Juliet cocked an eyebrow.

"Not him," said Sherlock.

Juliet and Sherlock pushed their way to the center of the arena. A boxing ring had been set up, and the gorilla was seated at a table in the middle of it. He was arm wrestling a slender female doll with dark curls and long eyelashes. She wore an elegant ball gown and appeared to be winning the match.

"Her," said Sherlock. He pointed to the woman. "Irene Adler."

"Sherlock Gnomes," the woman purred. She broke off the gorilla's arm and tossed it away.

"Wait, double or nothing?" begged the gorilla.

Irene snapped her fingers, and the big teddy bear ushered the gorilla away. Irene turned to face Sherlock. "You've got a lot of nerve showing your face around here."

"Hello, Irene," said Sherlock mildly. "You're looking well."

"A letter. You ended our engagement in a letter," Irene stormed.

Juliet took a step back. "You two were . . . engaged?"

"That might be a mild overstatement," said Sherlock.

"Don't you dare!" Irene hissed. "And now, after months of silence, you show up with this cheap porcelain thing."

Juliet raised her eyebrows. "I beg your pardon?"

"She's just my assistant," Sherlock said.

"Oh, I am *not* your assistant," Juliet shouted.

Irene smiled slowly. "Better get your stories straight."

"Irene, please," said Sherlock. "This is important.

This is one of yours, isn't it?" He held up the button.

"I don't know, Sherlock," Irene drawled. "There's an awful lot of buttons in this city."

"But precious few are used to pass coded messages through the ornamental underworld," replied Sherlock.

"Is that why you're here, Sherlock?" Irene's voice dipped dangerously low. "Did you come to bust me?"

Sherlock frowned. "You know why I'm here, Irene. You have something for me. A clue in my investigation."

"Of course you're only here for work. That's all you ever cared about." Irene stood up. "Sherlock Gnomes, it's time you got what's coming to you." She snapped her fingers and struck a pose.

"Are they going to smash us?" Juliet asked Sherlock.

"Even worse," Sherlock replied grimly. "She's going to sing."

Irene peeled down her fancy dress, revealing a dance costume underneath. Sherlock and Juliet listened as Irene performed a long song and dance number. Juliet didn't catch all the lyrics, but she got the impression that Irene was telling Sherlock

that she didn't need a man and was much better off without the wretched detective.

On the last beat of the song, the big teddy bear tossed Sherlock and Juliet outside and slammed the door behind them.

"Well, that was rather unpleasant." Sherlock brushed off his coat. "Irene must have the clue, because she was expecting me. She couldn't possibly have improvised such an elaborate song." He checked the sun, calculating the time. "She will need at least forty-two minutes to cool down—but we don't have the time."

Juliet banged on the door as hard as she could. "Listen up, doll," she cried. "You've got something I need, and I'm not leaving here without it. So, are you going to open up, or do I have to break your door down?"

Sherlock gasped. "Are you insane? You can't provoke Irene like that! She's an incredibly passionate doll. There's no telling what she'll—"

The door opened. The teddies emerged. "You can come in," the little teddy told Juliet.

As Juliet entered, the big teddy bear put a hand out and stopped Sherlock. "You can't."

Chapter 19

The teddies brought Juliet to a fancy dining room, where Irene sat waiting. She was at a table set for tea, wearing yet another stylish dress that went flawlessly with a lacy, wide-brimmed hat. "Here I thought garden gnomes were all overweight and bearded, but you're actually . . . cute. Hardly any facial hair at all." Irene picked up a teapot and stared icily at Juliet. "Would you like some tea?"

Juliet shook her head. "Um, no thank you." She wasn't sure how she would be able to convince Irene to help her, but she had to try something. "I, I just want—"

"I've often wondered what it's like to be a

gnome," Irene interrupted. "I mean, wearing the same red dress every day would be like a fashion prison for me. And living outdoors must be awful. Standing outside in the rain and the freezing cold. Like a dog."

Juliet lost her patience. "I really don't have time for this," she snapped. "Please, just hand over the clue."

Irene shook her head. "Work, work, work. Now I see why Sherlock chose you."

Juliet folded her arms. "It's not like that. Sherlock didn't 'choose' me."

"And he never will," said Irene. "With Sherlock, work always comes first. There's always another case to crack, another mystery to solve, another backyard of gnomes to rescue."

"You don't understand," Juliet protested.

"Oh, I understand perfectly," said Irene. "Because I forced Sherlock to choose. Me or the work. And if he didn't choose me, what makes you think he'll choose some common garden gnome?"

Juliet sprang to her feet. She was furious. "Enough!" she cried. "I don't care about Sherlock. He is the single most annoying gnome I've ever met. I wouldn't date Sherlock if he were the last gnome on Earth."

The teddies drew back, scandalized.

Juliet kept going. "I already have a partner. And he's nothing like Sherlock. Gnomeo is reckless and emotional and isn't obsessed with work. Gnomeo just wants to have fun . . . with me. He just wants to have fun with me. And he doesn't treat me like an assistant. He treats me like I'm . . ." She smiled, remembering. "Like I'm the toughest gnome in the garden. He believes in me. He loves me with all his heart. And if you asked him to choose between me and work or anything really, he'd choose me. *Every time.*"

Irene went silent. "A man doesn't make you strong," she said finally.

"You're right," Juliet agreed. "A man doesn't make you strong. But the right partner can make you *stronger.*"

Irene stared at Juliet, and the anger in her eyes melted into grudging respect. She was impressed by Juliet's strength. "All right. I'll give you want you want, but only on two conditions. First, you tell Sherlock this had absolutely nothing to do with him."

Juliet nodded. "And the second?"

"After you save the day, you come back here and tell me all about it." Irene rose up and extended her hand.

Juliet took the doll's hand and shook it. "You've got yourself a deal," she said.

A few moments later, Juliet was courteously escorted out of the dollhouse by the teddy bears. Before they closed the door, they handed her a card. "Thanks," she said.

Sherlock stood outside, completely in shock. "Irene gave you the clue?" He couldn't believe it.

Juliet sniffed. "Well, maybe she would have given it to you if you hadn't treated her so horribly."

"I didn't treat Irene horribly. I treated her the same way I treat everyone," Sherlock said.

"And you treat everyone horribly," Juliet informed him.

Sherlock stuck his hand out. "Can you just please stop talking and give me the clue?"

"Oh yeah, you're a regular Prince Charming." Juliet held out the clue, and Sherlock snatched it. It was an *M* card with scribbled writing on the back. Sherlock examined it, and then gave it back to Juliet.

"'You already know it's all about you. So what is the pattern in the final clue?'" Juliet read. She looked up at Sherlock. "This is it, isn't it? The last piece of the puzzle."

Sherlock didn't answer. He had already gone into his mind palace, analyzing the clues. "The patterns, the patterns, the patterns," he muttered. "Where are they leading us?"

As Sherlock put all the clues together, a familiar shape emerged in his brain. He brought his head up sharply. "Traitor's Gate! The old water gate entrance to the Tower of London. Where Watson and I solved our very first case," he mused. "But I don't remember it being an unpleasant experience." He frowned. "We're supposed to be there at precisely 8:43 p.m. Traitor's Gate is miles away. It will take us hours to get there."

"There has got to be a way we can get there in time," said Juliet.

"There is," replied Sherlock. "But it's a complete and total last resort." He tipped his head toward the ground.

Juliet heard the sound of a train rumbling underneath. "The Tube!" she gasped. "Let's go!"

Sherlock followed hesitantly. "You do realize how dangerous this is. We have, at best, a nine percent chance of surviving."

"Then nine percent it is," Juliet said determinedly. "Come on. We've got a train to catch."

Chapter 20

In the Victorian room, Gnomeo and the other gnomes were putting their plan into action. They were going to distract Reggie with a play while Gnomeo snuck out through the skylight.

The gnomes set up a stage using some blocks they found in the lost property box. Lady Bluebury went to an old Casio keyboard. She sat down and began to play an overture.

Paris took the stage. "Theater lovers, welcome," he announced. "Once upon a time, a beautiful princess was riding through the woods on her trusty steed."

Benny and Fawn appeared on the stage. Benny

was dressed as a princess, and was riding Fawn. "And now I'm typecast forever," the deer grumbled as he galloped across the stage.

Paris continued. "Suddenly, the princess came upon a frog who had been cursed by an evil witch."

There was a grunt, and Nanette was shoved onto the stage. "Ribbit. Ribbit," she said half-heartedly.

Reggie watched, riveted. Behind the gargoyle, Gnomeo was climbing up the fireplace using two garden trowels to dig into the bricks. The three goons clung to his ankles.

"And the only way, of course, to lift the curse was with a kiss from the princess," Paris said.

Benny leaned forward eagerly.

Nanette grimaced. "Surely there's another way to lift the curse. What if I kiss something else? Like a dung beetle? Or this guy?" She pointed to a toilet gnome.

"No," Paris said firmly. "A kiss from a princess is the only way to lift the curse."

Benny leaned in again.

Nanette backed away. "Okay, so how bad is this curse, exactly? I mean, are we talking permanent bad breath, or is it more serious, like a gluten allergy?"

Paris shook his head. "No, the curse is that you are a frog."

"Excuse me?" Nanette's voice rose an octave. "Since when is *this* considered a curse?" She walked off the stage. "I will not be a party to this antifrog rhetoric."

Without Nanette, the gnomes had to improvise. As Reggie started to turn away from the stage, Lady Bluebury shoved Mankini onstage.

"Then, suddenly, the evil Baron . . . Von . . . Mankini appeared," Paris blurted out.

Reggie turned back to the stage.

"The most . . . vile and . . . despicable villain that these lands ever did see," Paris stammered.

Mankini smiled innocently.

"Fortunately, the princess had her mighty horse. And he . . ." Paris trailed off as Fawn walked off the stage.

Meanwhile, Gnomeo had made it to the top of the fireplace. He hopped onto a roof beam and began to run across it, followed by the goons. He made it under the skylight, but it was too high for him to reach.

"So, now who will save the princess from the

baron's evil clutches?" Paris wailed miserably.

Gnomeo climbed up onto two goons. Standing on his tippy-toes, he was able to touch the skylight window with his fingertips, but he was still too short to open it.

"Who will save the princess?" Paris repeated desperately.

Reggie was getting bored. He was turning away from the stage when a deep rumbling voice cut through the air.

"Get away from the princess, you dirty rotten scoundrel!" Lord Redbrick jumped onto the stage.

"It was Prince Lord Redbrick," cried Paris, relieved.

"Indeed!" huffed Lord Redbrick. "And Prince Lord Redbrick knew, to *escape* the evil fiend, he had to grab that *third* pointy . . . *sword* and thrust it high into the air." Lord Redbrick thrust his imaginary sword into the air. Out of the corner of his eye, he saw Gnomeo's eyes brighten. He knew what Lord Redbrick was trying to tell him.

"Attaboy," Lord Redbrick whispered. Then he turned to Mankini. "Ha, ha! Now get out of here, Baron Von Mankini!"

Gnomeo grabbed the third goon and lifted him up, using his pointy hat to prop open the skylight.

"This prince guy is freaking me out," said Mankini.

"My hero!" cried Benny as Gnomeo disappeared through the window.

A moment later, a shadow descended. The goons tumbled back onto the roof beam as Ronnie flew through the skylight. She glared at the goons, and then looked down at the gnome stage. "What is all this?" she asked.

"They were putting on a show," explained Reggie.

"Yeah, well, show's over," roared Ronnie. She grabbed the goons and dumped them into the lost property box. Snatching gnomes left and right, she filled the box to the brim. Then she picked up an empty box and shoved it toward Reggie. "Boss needs these gnomes moved to the Tower Bridge," she snarled.

Lady Bluebury saw a blue hat poking through the skylight. Gnomeo raised his head for a brief moment and met her eyes. Then, he was gone.

Gnomeo had escaped.

Chapter 21

In the Baker Street underground station, Juliet and Sherlock slipped out of a heating duct and crouched behind a pillar. Sherlock whistled the sound of a text message. As the humans checked their phones, the gnomes hurried across the platform. They slipped down next to the tracks just as a sharp whistle came blasting through the tunnel. They pressed themselves against the wall as an enormous, terrifying train pulled into the station.

"Those front bumpers—they're our only chance of surviving this ride. Go!" Sherlock shouted.

The gnomes ran across the tracks and leaped onto the front bumpers of the train. There was a ding, and the train doors closed with a thud.

Sherlock and Juliet hung on for dear life as the train rumbled down the tracks. As they sped through the tunnel, a plastic bag caught on Sherlock's hat. It started to pull him off the bumper by sheer wind force. Sherlock reached up to remove the bag just as the train lurched. He slipped, and barely managed to grab on to the side of the bumper. He dangled, inches from the tracks below.

A sharp turn loomed ahead. Juliet gathered up her strength and swung herself onto Sherlock's bumper. She grabbed the detective and yanked him back up just before the turn.

The two gnomes squeezed together on the bumper. Just when they thought they couldn't hold on any longer, the train slowed and came to a stop.

"See?" panted Juliet. "Piece of cake."

"No, Miss Juliet." Sherlock looked grave. "There are eight more stops to go. I fear we're not going to make it."

Juliet's cursing was drowned out by a ding. The doors closed, and the train took off again.

Miles later, exhausted and half deaf, Sherlock and Juliet hopped off the train and sprinted to Traitor's Gate. On the gate, they saw a digital clock ticking down.

"We're nearly out of time. Hurry!" urged Sherlock.

They ran as fast as they could, but the clock hit zero before they had made it. Sherlock and Juliet arrived late, out of breath and gasping.

"Where are the gnomes?" Juliet asked.

"Show yourself, Moriarty!" Sherlock demanded.

Juliet wrenched open the door to Traitor's Gate and rushed inside. She found herself in a well-lit Victorian room scattered with blue and red paint chips on the floor. It was completely empty.

"Where are the gnomes?" Juliet cried.

Two winged shadows descended through an open skylight. Juliet looked up in horror as Ronnie and Reggie landed down in front of her. With a swipe, Ronnie had her firmly in her claws.

"Sherlock!" Juliet yelled. "Do something!"

Sherlock looked at Ronnie. Then he kicked the gargoyle, very lightly, on the shin.

"You've got to be kidding me," Juliet groaned.

Ronnie picked up Sherlock and threw both gnomes into a wooden box. As they got to their feet, they saw a bowler hat perched on top of a familiar figure. He was slumped on the floor with his head in his hands.

Sherlock gasped. "Watson?" For a second he stood frozen, hardly daring to breathe. Then he raced toward his partner and pulled him to his feet. He clasped one of Watson's hands and shook it over and over. "I've missed you, old friend," he said, his voice cracking for the first time in his life.

Watson tried to pull away, but Sherlock would not let go of his hand. He smiled. "How did you get here?"

"Moriarty's clues led us to Traitors' Gate, but then we were captured by these hooligans." Juliet shuddered. "We thought you were dead! How did you survive the fall at the museum? We heard you shatter on the ground."

"It was just a flower pot that fell," Watson said. "I managed to grab on to a ledge, but after the gargoyle took off with Gnomeo, it came back for me. I've been stuck in this box this whole time."

"Be quiet!" shouted Ronnie. She glared down

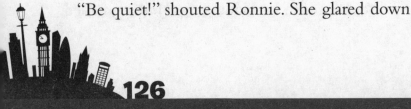

at the gnomes. "Let's go," she told Reggie. Holding the box between the two of them, the gargoyles lifted off through the skylight and into the open air. After what seemed like an eternity, the gnomes felt the box being set down, and the sound of wings flapping away.

As Juliet banged desperately on the side of the box, Sherlock sat staring at the tip of his shoe. It had a white speck on it from when he had kicked the gargoyle.

Juliet turned to the silent detective. "Sherlock!" she shouted.

Sherlock remained silent.

"For goodness sake! Will you just say something?" Watson pleaded.

"Limestone," Sherlock replied. "The substance on my shoe—it's limestone."

Juliet rolled her eyes. "He meant, say something *useful.*"

"I just did. The gargoyles lied. They're not from Traitors' Gate. So, if we can deduce where they're *really* from—"

"We'll find the gnomes," Juliet finished.

"That's why I kicked that gargoyle," Sherlock

explained. "To see, quite literally, what he was made of." He raised his foot and showed Juliet the white powder on his shoe. "Limestone," he pronounced. "Only nine percent of London's gargoyles are made of limestone. The gargoyles also reeked of salt. At first, I thought it was just the pungent musk of the Thames. But, here, taste my shoe."

Juliet shook her head. "Just keep going."

"The salt is from the gargoyles themselves, which means they must live close to the water." Sherlock put his hand on the side of the box. "Now, do you feel that?"

Juliet put her hand next to the detective's. She could feel the side of the box vibrating.

"It's the dull hum of a marine propulsion engine," Sherlock said. "Which means we're on a ship."

As if on cue, the deep blast of a ship horn sounded. The gnomes felt the box lurch from under them.

"From the sound of the horn, the HMS *Nimrod*, to be precise." Sherlock licked his finger and raised it above his head, testing the wind. "We've just set sail headed east, directly toward a structure which

is both on the water and protected by limestone gargoyles—"

"Tower Bridge!" Sherlock and Watson exclaimed together.

Sherlock staggered back. "Do you see? That's why he put us on this ship. We have to pass under the bridge."

Before Juliet could ask what on earth Sherlock was talking about, they heard slow clapping coming from the far side of the box. They looked over and noticed a hidden curtain.

Sherlock walked over and pulled back the curtain. Underneath, a cell phone was glued to the side of the box. And smiling straight at them from the glare of the cell phone screen was the sinister face of Moriarty.

Chapter 22

"Surprise, Sherlock!" Moriarty cackled. "Sorry to not be in touch. I was pretending to be dead. Oh, also, I hate you."

"Moriarty," Sherlock said. "How awful to see you."

"So I have been—I've been just peachy," Moriarty babbled. "Took up fishing, gave up fishing. It's really boring!" he said cheerfully.

Sherlock looked at the phone screen skeptically. "But . . . you're dead."

"Oh, you're talking about when the entire dinosaur fell on me!" Moriarty chuckled. "I survived the fall . . . and immediately began to plot your demise. But first, I wanted you to become the unwitting executioner of all the gnomes in London, which is why I kidnapped every single one of them. And when your pretty boat gets to the Tower Bridge, you will get to see them all die." Moriarty beamed. "So the game is not afoot or a hand or a leg, it's just over. And you lose. Bye-e-e-e!" He leaned over and pressed a button. The screen went blank.

Watson hung his head.

Sherlock closed his eyes.

Juliet stood very still. Then she drew back her foot and aimed it at the corner of the box. "Let's go save those gnomes," she said.

Three minutes later, the three gnomes had karate-kicked their way out of the box and made their way to the deck of the boat.

"We need to get off this ship," Sherlock said. "A naval destroyer should have—"

"Surveillance quadcopters," Watson finished. He pointed to a drone. "There!"

Juliet hopped onto the drone and grabbed the controls as Sherlock and Watson climbed on behind her. "I'll drive."

"Perhaps we should take this nice and slow," Sherlock said as the drone staggered into the air.

"My friends, my family, and the love of my life are in danger. I'm going to take this very, very fast," Juliet replied. She hit the throttle, and the drone took off like a shot.

Flying low through the fog, Juliet zoomed toward the Tower Bridge. As she approached, she saw a beloved figure with a blue cap running over the roof of the bridge. It was Gnomeo—with Moriarty and the gargoyles right behind him!

Juliet steered the drone upward. As she drew close, one of the gargoyles lunged out to grab Gnomeo.

Gnomeo ducked. Running as fast as he could, he took a mighty leap off the roof. His hand flew wildly in the air . . . and caught Juliet's hand.

"Gotcha!" Juliet said as she hauled Gnomeo onto the drone. "You deal with Moriarty," she told Sherlock and Watson. "Gnomeo and I will take care of the gargoyles."

Sherlock and Watson hopped onto the roof walkway, and Juliet gunned the engine, drawing the gargoyles farther upward. She shouted quick instructions to Gnomeo. When she reached the

very top of the bridge she hovered for an instant, just long enough for Gnomeo to leap down next to the bridge's powerful search beacon.

Juliet turned and plummeted toward the water. Ronnie and Reggie dove down after her. Right before she was about to hit the waves, she pulled up hard. The drone zoomed along, inches above the Thames, with the gargoyles in close pursuit.

A few seconds later the HMS *Nimrod* came into view, heading straight for the bridge. Flooring the pedal, Juliet raced the drone up the side of the ship and straight over the bow, where a cluster of human naval officers stood on the deck. As Ronnie and Reggie followed, the search beacon on the tower bridge turned . . . and shone straight at them.

Forced to freeze in place, the gargoyles dropped onto the ship. As the confused humans gathered around them, Juliet zoomed back to the bridge and landed next to Gnomeo, who was still pointing the search beacon steadily on the gargoyles.

Juliet leaped off the drone and gave Gnomeo a hug. "Gnomeo, I am so sorry."

Gnomeo clinked his head gently against Juliet. "I know. Me too."

The two gnomes shared a sweet, lingering kiss. "Now let's go get our friends back," Juliet said.

On the roof walkway, the two detectives were in trouble. Using his rolling pin, Moriarty had bashed away at Sherlock and Watson, knocking Watson to the edge of the bridge and cracking one of Sherlock's legs.

As Sherlock feebly raised his magnifying glass to ward off Moriarty's blows, the evil villain chuckled. "Oh, Sherlock," he said. "Did you really think you could defeat me? I am smarter than you. I am stronger than you. I am your superior in every way."

"Well, you're certainly more long-winded," Sherlock replied.

Moriarty sprang forward and knocked the magnifying glass out of Sherlock's hands. He spun and whacked Sherlock with his rolling pin, knocking him to his knees. "And now we've reached the end of our story. I always knew it was going to end like this." Moriarty raised the rolling pin high, ready to deliver the final, shattering blow. "With your inevitable destruction," he cackled.

Suddenly a cane flew through the air, knocking the rolling pin out of his hands. "No!" Moriarty screamed. He turned to find Watson standing at the edge of the walkway. Gnomeo and Juliet hovered in the drone next to him.

Watson darted forward and picked up his cane. "You're finished, Moriarty," he said.

Moriarty's eyes widened. Then his mouth curled into a sneer. "Well, then. My hat's off to you. Literally." He broke of his hat and hurled it straight into one of the drone's propellers.

The drone bucked, throwing Gnomeo and Juliet off it. With a screech, it crashed into the bridge, trapping the two gnomes beneath it.

"Hang on!" Watson yelled. He turned toward the destroyed drone and began to pull Juliet out of the rubble.

"Watson, behind you!" Juliet yelled.

Watson turned to see Moriarty skipping over.

"Hello!" said the villain. He picked Watson up and threw him over the edge of the bridge. Watson flung his hand out and barely managed to grab on to the ledge. He dangled helplessly, a hundred feet above the water.

"Okay, bye-bye!" Moriarty sang. He raised a foot to kick away Watson's hand.

"Come, Moriarty!" Battered and bruised, Sherlock limped over to his partner.

Moriarty raised his eyebrows. "Give it up, Sherlock. What are you going to do, depress me to death?"

Sherlock coughed. "Come dance with me," he said weakly. Gathering up the last of his strength, he threw himself onto Moriarty, hurling the two of them over the ledge.

As they fell, Watson reached down with his cane and lassoed Sherlock around the leg. He held Sherlock firmly as Moriarty continued to tumble down.

"Oh, big hairy bums," Moriarty groaned as he plunged into the Thames.

Watson and Sherlock climbed back onto the roof walkway and quickly freed Gnomeo and Juliet from the rubble.

Juliet brushed pieces of drone off Gnomeo's arm. "How did you know Moriarty was here?"

"When I was taken by the gargoyle, it brought me to a room with all the kidnapped gnomes."

Juliet nodded. "Traitors' Gate."

"I was able to escape," Gnomeo continued. "But before I did, I overheard the gargoyle saying that the boss wanted all the gnomes at Tower Bridge. So I got here as fast as I could, and found them locked up in one of the towers. Moriarty must have been interrupted before he could carry out whatever diabolical plan he had in mind." He grinned. "Shouldn't take more than a minute or two to free them."

Watson turned to Sherlock, still in disbelief that the detective had been willing to sacrifice himself for his partner. "You'd give your life for me?"

"Of course," Sherlock replied.

"Because you're the sworn protector of London's garden gnomes?" Watson asked.

Sherlock shook his head. "No. Because *we* are the sworn protectors of London's garden gnomes. Watson and Sherlock, partners in crime solving." He shook his head. "I'm sorry, old friend. I took you for granted for so many years. I should have realized that my—our—successes would never have happened without your hard work. We are true partners, equal partners, and we are strong and undefeatable precisely because we are a team."

Watson smiled warmly. "How could you possibly get on without me?" he said.

As Sherlock and Watson shook hands, Gnomeo held Juliet close. "Not bad, for our first week in London," he murmured.

Juliet smiled. "Hey, you're the one who wanted fun and adventure."

Gnomeo gazed deeply into Juliet's eyes. "With you. Always with you."

Epilogue

It was springtime in the new garden. What once was an overgrown plot had turned into a beautiful garden bursting with flowers, thanks to Juliet and Gnomeo's hard work.

"What a perfect day for your Seedling Ceremony," Lady Bluebury told Gnomeo and Juliet. "The garden looks absolutely gorgeous,"

Lord Redbrick took his daughter's hands in his own. "Juliet. I'm so proud of you."

Juliet smiled. "Thanks, Dad!" she said as everyone gathered around for the ceremony.

"On this, the first day of spring, Gnomeo and Juliet officially take leadership over the garden by planting a seedling together," declared Lady Bluebury.

"Benny, do you have the seedling?" Lord Redbrick asked.

"Yes, I do." Benny fished around in his pockets. "No, I don't."

"It's right here," sighed Nanette. She handed Gnomeo and Juliet a single, delicate little flower.

"Is this what I think it is?" Gnomeo asked.

Juliet smiled. "A Cupid's Arrow Orchid. Our flower."

Holding hands, they planted the seedling together.

"So, I guess this is officially our garden now," said Gnomeo.

"It is," replied Juliet. "And I'll never forget the most important thing in this garden . . . is you."

"Ooh, that was super cheesy," Gnomeo teased.

"No, it was extremely romantic," Juliet protested.

"Grade-A cheddar," Gnomeo pronounced.

Juliet shook her head, grinning. "Will you shut up and kiss me?"

As Gnomeo willingly complied, the gnomes cheered.

In the front row of the ceremony, Sherlock

watched Gnomeo and Juliet, astonished. "Watson! Do you see how they look at each other?" he mused. "Recalculating likelihood of breakup . . . at zero percent. Could that possibly be right?"

"Elementary, my dear Sherlock," said Watson. He smiled happily. "Elementary."